June 25, 1996

To Debby &
Yash

With Love,

Mort & Barbara

CITY BEAT

CITY BEAT

Stories From
the Heart
of
Cleveland

JAMES NEFF

John T. Zubal, Inc.
Publishers
1984

Published in the United States of America
John T. Zubal, Inc., Publishers

© 1984 by James Neff

ISBN 0-939738-55-4

First Edition

For Maureen

The hard necessity of bringing the judge on the bench down into the dock has been the peculiar responsibility of the writer in all ages of man.

    —Nelson Algren, *Chicago: City on the Make*

CONTENTS

Acknowledgements

First, I'd like to thank *The Plain Dealer* for permission to reprint my work. My gratitude goes to Publisher Tom Vail, Executive Editor Bill Woestendiek, Managing Editor Bob McGruder (who first pushed the idea for the column) and the City Editor, Bob McAuley. Additional thanks go to the copy desk, my safety net, and to my pals in the city room who alerted me to events unfolding on their beats.

Special thanks to our chief librarian, Patti Graziano, and her capable staff; they, too, perform on deadline. To the sources, tipsters, snitches, whistle-blowers, insiders and axe-grinders who keep me busy, keep it up.

I am also grateful to my readers. Sometimes cerebral, sometimes visceral, their responses to my columns are always helpful. My goal in writing "from the heart of Cleveland" has been to focus on the tremendous variety of humankind populating our town. The stories, happy and sweet, sad and grotesque, reflect life as it is on this reporter's city beat.

My love and appreciation go to my six brothers and sisters and to my parents, Dorothy and Charles Neff. And, above all, to Maureen, for her love and support.

J.N.
Cleveland
August 1984

1
ON THE STREET

Raiding Wash's

It was 4:15 Saturday morning. A man walked up to a ramshackle ghetto house.

A tall guy with a goatee blocked the doorway. "Hey, what's happening," the doorman said, patting down the man for guns and knives.

The man was clean. He strolled into Wash's, the famous after-hours joint and cheat spot at 5511 Ensign Avenue.

When the city goes to sleep and the bars close, Wash's place starts to make money. Despite several hundred raids on the place since 1941, Wash's has kept its doors open.

On Saturday, Wash's was crowded and dark and foul from cigarette smoke. In the middle room, amid the trash and empty beer cans, sat a second-hand juke box blasting out pounding, repetitious funk.

A fat lady in a blue dress at the bar sold cans of Bud for a buck. A few ugly hookers hit on some of the patrons. Nearby in the gambling room, six men sat at a table covered in maroon felt and played dollar-ante poker.

One of the players, a bearded guy with a southern accent, smoked marijuana and inadvertently flashed his cards as he tried to pass his smoke to the other players.

The old man running the game, Arthur Sanders, seventy-five, ignored the guy's patter and raked the house's 10 percent cut from each pot.

Wash's is named after its retired proprietor, Wash Carlton, a disabled man of seventy-one.

Wash's attracts some sleazy characters, but it also attracts blue-collar workers from the factories around E. 55th Street and Carnegie Avenue who want a beer after the third shift. And it attracts far-flung suburbanites looking for a walk on the wild side.

On Saturday, they got plenty of excitement. Around 4:30 a.m., the cops raided Wash's.

Undercover vice detectives and uniformed officers toting shotguns fanned out, turned off the jukebox and shut down the game. They arrested and handcuffed the gamblers, the bartenders and the doorman.

Then the Fourth District police ran warrant checks on everyone else. Seventeen people with outstanding warrants, from traffic violations to felonies, ended up in jail that morning.

A woman in a dirty blue bathrobe sat on a ratty chair and spat out her words. "I ain't going to jail without no (bleep)ing clothes," she told a cop. "No way, Jack. I ain't going to no jail without no clothes."

The woman, Mary Ackley, had an outstanding warrant for carrying a concealed weapon.

"Go ahead and get dressed," she was told.

This was the second time in eight days that Lt. William Stanley and his vice detectives had busted Wash's. Although Wash's is a nickel-and-dime operation, they had reasons for spending so much time on the place.

Two weeks ago, the body of David Mobley, twenty-six, was found near E. 88th Street and Cedar Avenue. The night he was killed he had told his mother he needed $5 because he was going to Wash's.

She gave him the money but begged him not to go. His body, bullet holes in the forehead and stomach, was identified February 8th. Homicide detectives have been stumped ever since.

The Fourth District vice squad hoped they could turn up information about the slaying by taking down Wash's. Police hoped that some of the after-hours habitués who were arrested might know something: whom Mobley was with, where he went afterwards, did he have an argument, whatever. Maybe they would volunteer information in exchange for favorable treatment.

Wash said yesterday he had heard of the killing and told police he would help them all he could.

"We get along fine," he said in his raspy voice, rolling a fat *El Producto* in his mouth. "I respect them. They're doing their job."

Wash certainly has kept them busy. He was arrested seventy-eight times between 1941 and 1976. Nearly all were misdemeanors for gambling and liquor violations. He pleaded guilty and paid fines of $100 to $200.

"I'm no fool," he said. "I know I'm violating the law, and I don't ask them [the police] to condone what I'm doing. But it's the only thing I know. I've been a handicapped man all my life."

In 1938, a half hour after he got married, Wash's "outside woman" stabbed him in the chest. He is paralyzed on his left side.

"I had to do something to eat," he insisted. "This was before welfare. So I started a little crap game. This was my way of eating, and I've never been on welfare.

"A fish needs water to swim in. If I quit operating, I quit eating."

February 21, 1983

The Doctor's hurtin'

At first, the Doctor pretends he doesn't hear the question. The hillbilly song on the jukebox isn't that loud, but the Doctor is sixty-nine years old. He can sidestep a question about his business, which is making sports book.

"The strike," he says, relenting after a moment. "Nobody's happy about it. The fans, the players, the owners. Nobody's happy about it. That's all I can say."

The owners are losing $38 million a week. The players are forfeiting $7 million a week. What the Doctor is losing, he won't reveal.

The Doctor admits his action is slow. Bettors still are wagering on college football and World Series games, but not with the relentless, weekly mania that makes pro football the national gambling vehicle.

"In the first place, nobody's got any money," Doctor explains patiently. "They need it for the household duties. Now there's nothing."

The Doctor is one of scores of bookies in town. He enjoys a reputation for fierce honesty. He's small-time; he rarely has to lay off big bets with the big bookies.

"I'm not the Syndicate," he says with a full-throated laugh. "I've only got a few customers left."

The Doctor looks like your favorite, kindly grandpa. He retains a full head of snow-white hair. With a fleshy pink face and a neatly trimmed white mustache, he reminds you of a greeting card version of a jolly Dutchman.

He is wearing black slacks, a gray sports coat and a black polo shirt buttoned to the collar. He knows everybody in the Euclid Avenue lounge.

"Hi, George," he says to a guy at the end of the bar. "I didn't know it was your birthday."

His clients will tell you about the Doctor. He was a cab driver. He retired in 1967 without pension benefits. He is one of the best gin rummy players in the city. He used to drink a lot, but you could never tell when he had a full snoot. He's been through half a dozen wives. Now he's living with a girlfriend.

"I wouldn't be able to live without it [bookmaking]," the Doctor goes on. "I get Social Security — $235 a month. Doesn't even pay the rent."

The big legal bookmakers in Las Vegas say they're losing 40 percent of their business, tens of millions of dollars, as the strike is prolonged. But the big Vegas bookies aren't worried about rent. Maybe they'll cut back on playing the stock market.

For the Doctor, the lost business is a direct hit on his wallet. He may not have the scratch to fix his 1971 Malibu, should it go lame again.

"No brakes, no windshield wipers now," the Doctor explains, chuckling at his predicament: a bookie who has to figure the weather odds before he drives. Getting caught in a rainstorm without wipers or brakes is a hairier gamble than $20 on Clemson's football team.

"I used to play the horses," the Doctor says with some understatement. Once he had made enough money hacking around in his cab, he'd flip up the "off-duty" flag and head for the race track.

"I'd play anything, everything," he says with a laugh. "I was always broke. I owed every loan company in town."

A sharp-looking older guy in a tweed sport coat was sitting two bar stools away. "You want another one, Doc?" the guy asks.

Doc glances down to the drained shot glass of Crown Royal and the half-filled tumbler of water.

"No, Jack," the Doctor replies. "I got to go downtown. I'll have a couple beers there and I'll be loaded. I've got to drive back."

The Doctor keeps a precise schedule. This way, his clients know when and where to reach him.

At 4 p.m., he stops for one drink in a tacky lounge on Euclid. He orders a jigger of scotch or a glass of Molson beer. It depends on his mood. Then he drives his 11-year-old Chevy to a bar in the Flats. He drinks two beers with his buddies, takes a few wagers, and drives back to his apartment in a Euclid Avenue rooming house by 6:30 p.m.

Last night, he made sure he got back in time to take three or four World Series bets. Nothing big, really. Maybe $20 here, $10 there.

"I never really had any really good times," the Doctor says, getting up from the barstool to head to the Flats. "I was always on the shorts. Sometimes, I hoped the game was called off" — he begins to laugh heartily — "or they'd find me in the river. . . .

"I'm too old," he says. "I'm gonna hit that dirt pretty soon."

The game is called off for now. Maybe the Doctor really likes it that way.

October 14, 1982

Ben's crazy oasis

It was a strange sight yesterday in the heart of the heart of the ghetto.

The guy they call Ben Crazy was planting shrubs and tamping down fresh sod along the narrow treelawn of E. 79th Street.

The E. 79th Street block between Hough Avenue and Chester Avenue is Ben Crazy's turf. He sweeps gutters clean. He paints curbs white. He mows vacant lots and rids them of trash.

At night he patrols his domain with a 12-gauge shotgun and a .25-caliber pistol. He is guarding two brick apartment buildings and a frame house he bought for $10 each. About one hundred feet north is the spot where the 1966 riots erupted.

A blue sign with white letters in front of one of his buildings reads: "The Reason Some People Don't Recognize Opportunity is It Sometimes Comes Disguised as Hard Work."

Welcome to a tiny oasis in a desolate swath known as Hough.

"I'm an ant, not a grasshopper," said the 59-year-old man whose real name is Ahara Ben Nez. "I'm out here working and everybody else is driving by in the big cars, making fun. They be drinking, smoking pot, saying, 'Look at the crazy fool.' When winter comes, they be starving and I'm all right."

Ben Crazy was standing on the sidewalk and wearing a blue jogging suit with blue running shoes and a blue warmup jacket bearing his first name, "Ahara," in gold letters. He is a tall, well-built man who speaks with a slight lisp through missing front teeth.

The 1942 graduate of East High School was known to his classmates as George Hocker. He played football and baseball and boxed. He learned bricklaying from his dad. Since then, he has added carpentry, masonry and plumbing to his skills.

He went to nursing school in Chicago and has worked at several nursing homes in the area. He discovered he couldn't hold a day job and guard his properties. So he quit his nursing job in 1970.

"See all those people?" Ben Crazy asked, pointing to church-goers at the corner. "They come here all dressed up, showing their clothes off, driving big cars. The rest of the week, the doors are locked up. If you're a bum or a wino, you can't get a loaf of bread. You gotta go to the Catholic churches."

If someone needs a meal or a place to flop, Ben Crazy takes care of him. He wants to breathe life into the neighborhood where he was reared.

With hard work, he hopes to turn his buildings into federally subsidized apartments for the elderly and mentally handicapped. He has never received a government grant or welfare.

"Everybody wants something for nothing," he said. "I never took no handout. Then I couldn't set the example I wanted to show. If one man can do it, why can't somebody else do one property?"

At times, his one-man battle seems to be a futile one. Vandals have torn out his shrubs and broken his windows. Outsiders dump rubbish on his vacant lots. He has fallen thousands and thousands of dollars behind on property taxes.

The drug houses and after-hours joints that infest his neighborhood are a magnet for crime. But he doesn't have to scare off thieves much anymore.

"The word went out, 'He's crazy, he'll shoot ya,' " he said. "That's why they call me Ben Crazy. Just like the snake says, 'Don't tread on me.' "

His biggest problem has been his occasional tenants. They have raped his buildings.

They don't pay rent. They move out at night and steal the radiators and copper plumbing and anything else of scrap value. They pollute the environment on his oasis.

Right now, Ben Crazy has only four tenants, none of whom pays. They can't afford it or else know he's a soft touch.

One tenant is a General Motors retiree, seventy, who lives on the first floor of a building. Ben Crazy says the man is drinking himself to death.

"I watch his health," Ben Crazy said. "I take him to the doctor, and he doesn't even say thank you. He cusses me out, and I still do it. I'm too much of a humanitarian."

Despite his good works, Ben Crazy is not a man of religion, at least not organized religion.

"They're all fronts," he will tell you. Instead, he erects signs with inspirational sayings on his property. "God Made Me Do It," says one. "Faith Hope Charity," reads another.

When the rain started again yesterday afternoon, Ben Crazy's visitor got off the street and into his car to leave.

"This rain doesn't bother me," Ben Crazy said. "I was up all last night laying sod. I'll have this finished tomorrow."

May 2, 1983

Shooting up Billy

He had hocked the gun to the woman who ran the bar. Now he needed it back. Billy had to take care of business.

He limped out of the Collinwood tavern, his heavy boots scuffing the ice, and climbed into a beat-up Buick he liked to drive on missions like this one.

Billy pulled the .38-caliber revolver out of the waist of his blue jeans, loaded it and concealed it in a red stocking cap on the front seat. He was glad she had let him borrow the gun for an hour or two.

Minutes later, about noon, he eased the car to a trash-strewn curb in front of one of the orange-brick housing projects on E. 55th Street.

The men hanging out on the corners looked at Billy and guessed his game. This was Brick City. When you see a white face under a black beard and cowboy hat, you know what the man wants. Billy had come to score.

He tucked the gun in his pants and pulled his black leather coat around his waist. Putting a swagger in his walk, his head scanning slowly left to right, Billy made his way to a second-floor apartment.

A thin old woman, her gray hair twisted into a braid, rested on a stool in front of a window facing the street. An exposed radiator hissed a few inches behind her. Except for an old TV and a ratty piece of couch, the room was empty, its concrete floors splashed with grime.

"Keep an eye on my car," Billy told the woman.

Billy found her son, Lewis, in a room with a mattress and a wood crate for a table. This was their shooting gallery.

Billy pulled his coat aside, displaying the .38 to Lewis, an act of ritual and protection. In the drug world, there's no such thing as a friend.

"You know I don't (bleep) around, Lewis," Billy warned.

"Sho' you right."

"Anything jumps off, some (bleep) tries to take my dope, I get serious."

"Sho' you right."

They got in the car and drove a block to a pale green motel. Billy gave Lewis $35 to buy two pills from their connection.

"Make sure he does me right," Billy said.

"I take care of you."

Minutes later, Lewis was back in the car.

"Everything straight?" Billy asked.

"Sho' you right." They drove quickly back to the apartment. They were anxious to get high.

"I was gonna buy your mom a bottle of wine," Billy said.

"That's OK."

Back at the dreary flat, Billy gave the old woman a bill and said, "Keep your eye on my car."

Then Billy and Lewis went to the bedroom.

A skinny kid with straight hair hanging down his back was lying shirtless on the mattress. He had an arm tied off at the shoulder with a black strip of cloth. He was having a hard time shooting up.

Lewis held the black cloth and the junkie found a vein in his armpit and hit the line.

"Get out of here, man," Billy told the kid. "I want privacy."

After the kid left, Billy told the room: "I can't stand guys who shoot in their armpit. It makes me sick."

They took off their shirts. They didn't want to get the sleeves spotted with blood.

Billy crushed a Dilaudid pill into a bottle cap and squirted in hot water from a half-filled syringe. He cooked the cap with a cigarette lighter until the powder dissolved. Through a piece of cotton, he pulled the dope into the syringe.

He tied off his arm, found a vein, jabbed the needle and hit the plunger.

"Bet you never saw me get off that fast," he said.

Lewis didn't answer. He was busy doing the same.

Billy felt the drug grip him. He sat on the mattress for five minutes, enjoying the rush. Then he quickly put on his shirt and jacket and left.

"I don't know why I do it," he said outside. "I don't have a Jones [habit] going."

Not yet, anyway.

Billy was back in Brick City two nights later. He was parked when a police car pulled up.

"Put your hands on the dashboard," he was told. "We know who you are. What are you doing here?"

"Waiting for a friend," Billy said.

"We know what you're doing," one cop said. "You're gonna get killed down here."

Names have been changed in this column.

January 30, 1984

Darryl X's advice

He calls himself Darryl X. He was dressed in Army surplus fatigues and sitting in a 24-hour downtown restaurant yesterday afternoon. A medium-built black man, Darryl X calls himself a "hard-times consultant."

"Instead of having a big Continental, I'd rather have a big gun and a big sandwich," he said.

Darryl X is a survivalist. He preaches a message to his brothers and sisters: how to live through hard times by bartering, budgeting, growing your own food, working in the underground economy, even raising rabbits for food, if necessary.

"I know people raising chickens and slaughtering them," he said. "I know it sounds far out. . . . Rabbits are legal and easier."

Darryl X also teaches you how to arm and protect yourself in case of a riot, a food shortage, a natural disaster or a criminal attack.

"I'm just trying to reach other folks," he said yesterday. "I'm talking about self-sufficiency. I'm trying to give people an alternative to violence and desperation and death."

The city's underclass today faces desperate times: East Ohio Gas Company is raising its prices 40 percent; meteorologists say this winter will be one of the toughest; supply-side Reaganomics is revealing itself to be a cruel hoax.

In the face of all this, Darryl X delivers a message of hope. He tells you how to stay warm with kerosene heaters, how to purify water, where to buy an emergency dental kit that can replace fillings, how to start an urban garden, how to reload ammunition, and so on.

"This could help you in any situation," he said. "People talk about running to the voting booth to solve their problems. That's fine. But even if you vote in who you want, it's going to take time to get the things you're after. By having the things I mentioned, no matter who's in charge or what's going down, you're ready."

Survivalism, a burgeoning movement during these tough times, is the concern, generally, of the well-to-do. For example, a doomsday retreat in the north California hills charges $12,000 for membership and $300 in monthly dues for the security of its remote bomb shelter and year's supply of firewood and freeze-dried food. Ninety-nine percent of the readers of *Survive,* the Bible of the movement, enjoy a median income of $25,000 to $30,000.

But Darryl X is preaching self-sufficiency for ghetto blacks, the first to suffer in a hard-hit economy.

"Our people, in general, as a mass of people, feel [first] the economic effects of factory closings," he said. "But black people in general are the last ones to think about it. I'm at the frontier for black people, as far as this movement goes."

Most survivalists fear the future. Darryl X believes his advice has direct, practical application today. For $5, he sells a 25-page booklet that explains survival techniques and lists suppliers of survival gear. He tosses in free consulting.

"So many people around me are suffering," Darryl X said. "I've prepared myself. I don't have to suffer. I want to teach other people things I've learned. It's more or less out of compassion for other people. This has been a turning point in my life. It gives me more purpose. I committed myself now to this movement. It gives me more strength to keep on living."

Like all survivalists, Darryl X is secretive. If the have-nots know he has stashed a year's supply of food, then he believes he'll be attacked during a crisis. Darryl X will not reveal his last name or his address. He did admit yesterday he is twenty-five years old, graduated from a Cleveland high school, worked at the Brook Park Ford Motor Company plant, and lives near University Circle with his wife and two children. He is unemployed and also hides his identity because he fears White Power nuts.

"The Nazis and the Ku Klux Klan talk about fighting a race war," he explained. "If they hear about blacks storing food and guns, they might think we're out to get them."

When things were good at Ford four years ago, Darryl X sometimes earned $900 to $1,200 a week with overtime. He squandered the money foolishly, buying expensive clothes and dining and drinking recklessly at Swingos and the Pewter Mug.

Then, about two years ago, he was reduced to living like a hobo, sleeping in rapid stations and scrounging for food. These experiences, he said, prepared him to teach urban survival.

"It's all about knowledge," he said. "And knowledge is the great-est thing. Knowledge is power. It makes you more independent."

October 18, 1982

Passing through

An old man in shabby clothes lay on the Greyhound bus station floor yesterday evening. He clutched $85 in one hand and held the other over his heart. He moaned and cried and banged his head gently against the door to the depot's security office. His breath filled the tiny office with the stench of cheap wine.

Three policemen looked down at the old guy, Earl Donaldson, whose 82nd birthday is tomorrow.

"I was going to arrest him, so he faked a heart attack," said Lt. Leroy Brinkhoff, at once perplexed and amused. "Let's call C-med."

A city emergency medical team showed up quickly, strapped Donaldson onto a stretcher, took his blood pressure and began to wheel him out. "You haven't been drinking?" a C-med asked Donaldson.

"He'll probably live longer than any of us," Brinkhoff marveled. "He's pickled. He's well-preserved."

Brinkhoff recognized Old Earl. He's one of the bus station's many characters. Yesterday, most of the regular cast was there.

On Sunday, the Greyhound station has a rhythm of its own. By evening, the college kids are lined up for the express buses back to Bowling Green, Ohio State and other campuses. Their fresh young faces and clean blue jeans and colorful parkas are in sharp contrast to the sly looks of the riffraff operating on the depot's fringes.

The bus station is like a beehive. Except for the winos like old Earl, no one is relaxed. Everyone is either moving on, working his shift or hustling.

Mark is one of the hustlers. He likes the college crowd. He operates near the front door, selling small packets of marijuana, some of it bogus, some of it real.

Mark is a slim 22-year-old who wears a black leather jacket and a black goatee. He never made it through Shaw High School. He got stoned too much.

"You get high?" he asked a young man in blue jeans and cowboy boots yesterday. "I got some reefer."

He reached into his jeans and pulled out a brown envelope the size of two tea bags.

"This is a good dime bag," Mark went on. "I got to sell two more today, then I'm gone. I got a friend who needs the money."

Inside the security office, a color snapshot of Mark adorned the wall next to a bulletin board checkered with mug shots.

The inscriptions under the dozens of mug shots told different stories: "Mental mental mental," read one. "Three-card monte operator," said another. "Pick-pocket," warned a third.

Mark's mug shot revealed him to be a sweetheart. It showed he was busted on Valentine's Day for possession of marijuana and criminal trespass.

"Most of the time, his stuff is junk that he sells as dope," said Brinkhoff. "He'll roll oregano in egg whites and sell it as hash. These people are easy marks. By the time they know they're ripped off, they're on the bus somewhere. What are they going to do? Tell us they bought some bad drugs and we should arrest the guy?"

Actually, the Greyhound station is safe if you keep to yourself. The hustlers hope that boredom and being in a strange place will lead you to let down your guard, to do something you wouldn't try on your own turf.

Fifteen off-duty Cleveland policemen work four shifts a day, seven days a week, overseeing this hubbub. It beats working an eight-hour shift standing in a bank lobby.

The policemen here see all kinds.

On Thursday an alert patrolman, Lou Catalino, recognized Anthony Roden, an accused cop-killer on the loose from a psychiatric center who was traveling under the name of James Frank. The SWAT team came and captured Roden.

One year ago, John Hinckley Jr. switched buses here on the way to Washington where he tried to kill President Reagan with a cheap handgun.

The jitneys — unlicensed cab drivers — work Chester Avenue near the front door of the depot. Near the bank of pay phones, the well-dressed and well-versed con men work the pigeon drop, a sting operation.

Pimps prowl for runaway teen-age boys and girls, buying them a meal and supplying the sympathy they didn't get at home. If the

pimps are lucky, they can turn the teen-ager out to pasture in a
week or so. "We don't see pimps that often," Brinkhoff said.
"Maybe it's so subtle we don't notice it."

Brinkhoff, when on duty for the Cleveland Police Department,
is a desk jockey — a platoon commander in the First District. It's
a boring job.

"There's variety here," Brinkhoff said yesterday. "And you can
help people. Yesterday, I carried a crippled kid off the bus. I'm
here because it's an interesting place to work."

April 5, 1982

Stalking the Angels

The dark awning in front of the white house at 6621 Edna Avenue bears a helmeted death's head.

An American flag flaps on a pole high above a row of shiny black Harleys parked neatly along a curb.

You're in Hell's Angels territory on the near East Side.

Inside the house, you find a pool table, a bar, modern couches and stuffed chairs, a weight-lifting room, a kitchen with appliances and a commercial ice maker.

Along the walls hang huge photos of brother bikers who died wearing their colors. Whitey — smashed by a car. Beetle — mysteriously blasted off his bike on a highway in Iowa. Dirty George — shot by his girlfriend. And so on.

Eugene Padavick, president of the Cleveland Hell's Angels chapter, was resting a thick, tattooed forearm on a giant glass jar filled with coins and folded bills. His T-shirt said, "Hell's Angels are Americans."

"We're highly visible," Padavick said. "We're not hiding somewhere and driving in dark-windowed cars. We're sitting on two-wheeled motorcycles. We got our patches on our backs."

The Department of Justice is waging war on the notorious Hell's Angels.

"Motorcycle gangs are an up-and-coming criminal force in the United States," Sean McWeeney, chief of the FBI's organized crime section in Washington, has said. "These are very strong groups, very powerful forces."

Hell's Angels run drug and prostitution rings, fence stolen motorcycle parts and perform contract hits for the Mob, officials say.

"We enjoy each other's company here," said Padavick, defending the thirty or so men he calls his brothers.

"They [federal agents] throw all the crime in Cleveland on us. They've got all the organized crime people in jail. So now they have to have a focal point and we're a focal point."

Actually, the Hell's Angels became a center of attention in courtrooms here in the past year because a 13-year-member, Clarence "Butch" Crouch, turned government informant.

Crouch, an admitted pimp, pusher and hitman, told federal agents he was "tired of all the killing" and that he could make cases against his former brothers. Crouch agreed to plead guilty to manslaughter, serve time and be paid $1,245 monthly as a federally protected witness.

So far, it's been a bad deal for the government. Crouch has figured as star prosecution witness in five murder trials. He's 0 for 5.

One: Crouch said Hell's Angel Jack Gentry murdered a man, "rolled his bones," as an initiation requirement for the Hell's Angels. A Toledo jury found Gentry not guilty.

Two and three: Crouch said Angels Richard Amato and Harold Chakirelis bombed a house, killing three. A Common Pleas judge dismissed the charges, saying prosecutors failed to produce enough evidence.

Four: Crouch said Andrew Shission, to join the gang, gunned down rival biker Buddy Sunday. A Common Pleas judge dismissed aggravated murder charges after prosecutors rested their case.

Five: Crouch said he was the triggerman who killed an Akron man, mistaken for a rival biker, and Shission was an accomplice. An Akron jury didn't believe Crouch and acquitted Shission.

"If we're doing all this, where are all the convictions?" Padavick demanded.

Bill Wood, head of the Alcohol, Tobacco and Firearms office here, countered: "We don't classify them as a group of Boy Scouts. We have every reason to believe the group is involved in criminal activity."

Why have the cases fallen apart? Were they too flimsy to bring to court in the first place?

"The type of information Crouch was privy to was about crimes that happened a long time ago," said Wood. "We make the best presentation we can. . . . We're continuing our investigation."

So is the FBI.

Padavick, an ironworker, packs 195 solid pounds on a 5-foot-7 frame. As he talked to a visitor, several Hell's Angels gathered in the clubhouse to listen and to chime in.

"This has been a good year," Padavick mused. "It's been good for setting the record straight. We had an opportunity to go to court. All our brothers are home and out of jail."

The burly biker measured his words, paraphrasing Nietzsche: "That which don't kill us, makes us stronger."

February 2, 1984

Sidewalk business

When Gregory Perkins arrived at King's Bar yesterday, the sidewalk out front was thick with thieves.

There was Candy Man, tall and thin, in beige slacks and a matching cap. Candy Man sells a rainbow assortment of pills, hence his nickname.

Leaning against a pay phone was Jeffrey, a thin young male with high heels, tight jeans and painted lips. Jeffrey, a female impersonator, is a part-time prostitute.

A bearded guy flashed bills to a fat woman wearing a white dress and a white scarf. She took the money, put it in a pocket, looked around, then handed him some pills.

Perkins, a broad-shouldered dude in a gray leather coat and a brown felt hat, strolled back and forth in front of King's Bar, 2197 E. 55th Street. The sun was warm, the day was young, and he had competition — half a dozen pushers had been working the area yesterday.

If you had been watching through binoculars from a nearby police surveillance vehicle, you would have seen Perkins make three sales in less than an hour.

The sidewalk in front of King's is a hot spot for drugs and a trouble spot for police. It's practically a hiring hall for hoods. Police say three of the men who assaulted Councilman Lonnie Burten and his associates were recruited from King's.

Only two days ago, another body was discovered on the sidewalk outside King's. Police say the deceased was a pill peddler and stick-up man with a long criminal record. He was shot twice in the chest with a pistol. A blast from a shotgun took off the left side of his face.

From March 30, 1981, to March 30, 1982, the Fifth District

made 184 arrests in or in front of King's — sixty-five for drug violations, eleven for carrying a concealed weapon, nine for theft, three for aggravated robbery, one for homicide, two for felonious assault — the list goes on.

"It's just a cesspool of humanity that needs to be cleaned up," said the Fifth District commander, Capt. Anthony J. Slezak.

The Fifth District is only six square miles. Last year, police assigned there made 2,775 violent crime arrests, more than in any of the other five police districts.

Rufus Harris owns King's Bar and another rough spot, Cafe Society, on E. 105th Street near St. Clair Avenue. Last spring, in front of Cafe Society, a guy smacked Harris' wife, Aileen, as Harris pulled up in his car. Harris blew the sucker away with a single shot from a .38-caliber revolver. Harris was acquitted of murder.

Harris, sixty-three, wants to keep King's and the flophouse above it. His lawyer, Ken Fisher Jr., was in Columbus two days ago at the State Liquor Control Board to fight an attempt by police to pull Harris' liquor license.

"I can't handle the street," Harris moaned. "What can I do? I don't control the sidewalk. . . . You go and you work hard and you try to make a living and look what you get. They drive off all my street business. . . . How can I move when I'm damn near broke?"

Lt. Bill Vargo, the smooth-spoken boss of the Fifth District Detective Bureau, told a different story:

"He must be doing OK since he's fighting so hard to keep it. . . . If those people weren't at that bar, who would go there? Nobody. That's the only clientele he attracts. He'd be cutting his own throat if he threw them out. How could a businessman do that?"

Yesterday it was learned that Harris won. He gets to keep his license. The police lost.

The liquor control board members "bury their heads in the sand," Vargo said. "They refuse to acknowledge that the area in front is as much a part of the bar as the barstools inside. . . . Once a man secures a liquor license in this state, it's damn near impossible to get it pulled. It's like a federal judgeship."

Gregory Perkins was sitting in his car when detectives Ron LaRich and Neptali Ramos pulled up. The cops patted him down and searched an arm's length around him. LaRich reached under the dashboard and found a leather pouch. It was filled with pills. They made an inventory later: fifty-nine Percodans, twenty-seven Preludins, thirty-seven Talwins, sixty-five pyrobenzamines, about $1,500 worth of uppers, downers and opiates. Talwin and pyrobenzamine, nicknamed "Bs and Ts" or "bottoms and tops," produce a heroin-like high when mixed three to one and injected.

Later, Perkins called his bail bondsman from the phone booth in the Fifth District's lock-up.

"Hey, baby," he spoke into the phone. Then he looked up and saw some visitors. "Hold it. . . ." He covered the mouthpiece with his ring-festooned fingers.

"Gregory, how much do the Talwins go for on the street?" he was asked.

"Fo' dollars," he replied. "I sell my Ts for four and my Bs for eight."

April 1, 1982

Pee Wee's plight

Pee Wee poked his head out of the shanty into yesterday's bright afternoon sun.

"No ribs," Pee Wee said. "It was too windy Saturday. I didn't want to get no sand on anybody's barbecue."

He walked out the door of Pee Wee's Little Country Store onto the glass-strewn parking lot at E. 66th Street and Hough Avenue. "I got some shoulder," he said. "Come on inside."

Pee Wee stands 5-feet-4. His brown eyes flash a hard-earned wisdom that comes from forty-four years of hustling to support a family. His real name is Glover Treadwell and he wears a black cowboy hat, blue jeans and a jean jacket with an embroidered longhorn steer on each shoulder.

"I just got style," he explained. "I'm from Tennessee."

For the last four years, when the weather breaks, Pee Wee has run a tiny store and barbecue joint in one of the poorest sections of Hough. He constructed and wired the shanty using mostly salvaged material.

The colorful clapboard shack with homemade signs and four boarded windows is about six feet wide and twelve feet long.

Inside, a large propane tank fuels a small double gas burner that rests on the floor. The burner heats the store and boils the water in which he pre-cooks his ribs. Narrow shelves are sparsely lined with the sundries he sells: cigarettes, rolling papers, soft drinks, aspirin, candy, cookies and so on.

He proudly showed off his three licenses — vendor's, cigarette and food handling. "I don't make no big thing," he said. "I don't make no money."

An old refrigerator occupies one corner, but Pee Wee has no electricity to run it. Until last week, he lived next to the store in a ramshackle three-story house. Pee Wee had rigged an electric line in from the house to the store to power a refrigerator, a radio, a tape player and a big plastic *Pepsi* sign.

He lived in that house for nearly three years, the last two without gas and hot water. The owner stopped paying for gas, but still charged rent. Pee Wee and the first-floor residents stuck it out, moving in with relatives during the winter and migrating back in the spring.

Last week, someone set the house on fire. The next day, scavengers ripped out the copper plumbing and took what was left of the furniture Pee Wee had locked up in his third-floor apartment.

"And two weeks ago, somebody stole my car," Pee Wee said. "I had a 98 Olds. I'm jus' holdin' on."

Pee Wee's plight is not unusual in the Hough area, where 86 percent of the people, most of them blacks, survive on some form of subsidized income. But the warm weather this weekend brightened their dreary picture. Utility bills will drop dramatically.

And now Pee Wee can barbecue outside. By summer, his chairs and tables should be filled with neighborhood folks hanging out, listening to music, eating barbecued shoulder sandwiches and pork ribs and cole slaw, and drinking brown-bagged beer.

"Oh, it's done cooled down around here," Pee Wee explained. "But it's still rough. You got to watch yourself."

Pee Wee said this west end of Hough has cooled down because many abandoned houses have been torched. The houses were temporary homes and meeting spots for junkies, thieves and assorted troublemakers who sold drugs and fought with one another.

He stood up without crouching inside his tiny store and pointed in different directions as he listed the houses that had burned down since January in a two-block area surrounding his store.

"There's been one, two, three, four, five, six, seven that I know of," he said. Three in nine days. All that's left are level lots crisscrossed by fresh bulldozer tracks in the sandy soil.

Pee Wee isn't sure who torched the houses — he says maybe the owners, maybe junkies seeking to steal the copper plumbing. The result is a welcome one.

"They burned the rats out," he said. "I call them rats. Now they got to go to some other neighborhood."

Pee Wee was carrying water in a railroad crew when he was thirteen. Two years later he hopped a freight with friends and ended up in Toledo. They stayed in flophouses for 25 cents a night. He has picked potatoes with migrants, done odd carpentry and plumbing jobs, and he has a sixth grade education.

"I've been on the hustle all my life," Pee Wee said. "I like to do something for myself if I can. I like to look back on something I did. It gives me enjoyment."

He runs the only store in Hough that sells candy for a penny. If a group of kids stops at the store and one doesn't have a penny, Pee Wee gives him a cookie or a piece of candy.

"I always give them something," he said. "That's why they love me. They say, 'Give me some candy, Mr. Pee Wee.' Next time they come back and pay me. They're nice kids in this neighborhood."

March 15, 1982

The hate and heat

When Andre Hicks was a baby, his aunt nicknamed him Tuffy. He is twelve now and lives in Glenville and has some street smarts.

Tuffy knows, for instance, that he shouldn't get caught riding his bike in white areas of Collinwood. What Tuffy does not know is his Cleveland geography.

He and a friend were pedaling back from Euclid early Sunday evening. They took a short cut from Euclid Avenue to St. Clair Avenue by cutting down London Road, entering into the turf of some clannish Italian-Americans.

"Two white boys started chasing us," Tuffy recalled. "We know Collinwood is a bad area. We didn't know that street was so rowdy."

" 'Nigger, you better get out of here,' " Tuffy said he was told. And moments later, "You ain't gonna make it." Tuffy's friend got away. Tuffy didn't.

An Italian woman was ironing in her living room. She heard a tussle and looked out.

"Here was this black kid passed out in the driveway, jus' like a beat-up muffler fall offa car," the woman said. "No one lif' a finger to help him. No one and jus' the week before, the priest was reading a sermon about the Good Samaritan."

She lives alone, except for her teenage son, and does not want her name used.

"I saw his face," she said. "His nose was bleeding. His heart was beating so fas'. All he saw were white faces. I said, 'Nobody gonna hurt you in my house.' "

A phone call was made and Tuffy's brother and friends drove over and got him. Then they circled the area looking for Tuffy's assailants. They found some whites, got out of the car and punched them. So it goes in Collinwood, where hate, heat and beatings have brought racial tension to a head this summer.

"There's a lot of racial tension," Councilman Michael Polensek was saying. "We've had assaults, car thefts, unfortunately carried out by blacks. You've got [white] people who feel it's being done on purpose. Mix that with high unemployment and the heat of the summer. People are frustrated, angry.

"There could be a riot," Polensek went on. "It could be one of the few cases in the country of a white neighborhood rioting. This shooting the other night has a lot of people upset. There's a lot of people looking for bear out here."

Thomas Necastro, eighteen, who is white, was shot driving west on St. Clair around 11 p.m. on July 12. He said three blacks walking in the area with a stick made racial remarks to him. He said he pulled to the curb, got out and warned the three to get out of the neighborhood or they'd get hurt.

The three cursed him. One whipped out a gun and shot twice, wounding Necastro in the left side.

The Collinwood neighborhood has a west side and an east side, with blacks on one side, whites on the other. Racial violence is no stranger to Collinwood. Things flare up and cool down without reason.

The Mason-Dixon line of Collinwood is E. 152nd Street. Polensek's ward is east of E. 152nd and is 93 percent white, mainly Italians, Croatians and Slovenians. West of 152nd is all-black Ward 10, represented by Councilman Larry Jones.

Jones doesn't believe the situation is as tense as Polensek feels it is. "I'm not trying to minimize the problems," Jones said. "Most of the stuff occurs east of 152nd."

The violence has a familiar pattern: blacks venturing in the evening into white parts of Collinwood get harassed, jumped or shot at by white thugs, mostly young men. Blacks regroup and retaliate, crossing back into east Collinwood in search of the assailants. Mostly the innocent get hurt.

One was Claudia Stockboe, a 29-year-old black Euclid woman. Last Saturday at 11:30 p.m., while riding a moped east on St. Clair near E. 175th Street, she noticed four white men in a green sedan following her. She said she was shot in the arm. She dumped her moped and ran. A guy got out of the car and drove off with her bike. Police are still investigating.

"It's really gonna be a bad situation if it continues," said a detective in the Sixth Police District. "Anytime you keep seeing these reports come in, you know something's up."

Capt. Robert Cavell, Sixth District commander, disagreed: "These are isolated incidents."

Collinwood residents say they are sick of news stories that point out hostility between whites and blacks in the area. Collinwood has not cornered the market on hatred.

Some insist reporting about racial tension fans the foul feelings, but truth can never hurt. It's rumors and ignorance that fuel the frustrations that goad people into base acts.

"Rumor is out that a black policeman came out behind a building and did the shooting [of Necastro]," Polensek said. "Rumors are a big problem. All kinds of rumors are floating at this time."

That rumor proved to be false.

The sons and daughters of the earlier mentioned Good Samaritan woman have been jumped by blacks, too.

"When it happen to my kids, I didn't blame all blacks," said the woman who was sitting on a couch next to her 18-year-old son. On the wall were pictures of the Pope and the Last Supper.

Her son interrupted: "I'm telling ya, mom, the black people are worse. Don't tell me they don't know where Collinwood is."

Her son hangs around Mandalay Pool, a city swimming pool that blacks are afraid to frequent because white toughs enforce it as their turf.

"If I drove down Euclid Avenue, I'd get clipped," he insisted. "They'd be shooting at me left and right."

The woman wondered about Tuffy, the black boy whose bloody face she wiped clean.

"This little boy," she said. "I hope he doesn't grow up with hate in his heart."

July 21, 1983

A future stolen

The day thieves broke into her classroom and stole the last of the felt-tip markers, Kecia Smith, twelve, decided to take action.

She called her best friend, Vanessa Jarvis, also twelve, and together they composed a letter about problems at their ghetto grade school.

"There have been too many robberies at our school," reads the letter, perfectly spelled and punctuated. "They have taken things we need to learn with. . . . Can you help us find the people who make us have a miserable education?. . . Why can't the police do something about it?"

Of Cleveland's eighty-eight elementary schools, Kecia's school, Daniel E. Morgan Elementary School at 1440 E. 92nd Street, is hit the hardest by burglars and vandals. Since September, thieves have taken seven cassette recorders for Morgan's THINK reading program, one television set, one duplicating machine, two sound projectors, several film strip projectors, hundreds of markers, books, tablets and supplies, eight wall clocks, a stove and a refrigerator, among other things.

Windows have been smashed dozens of times, and papers and books have been strewn about the classrooms.

The neighborhood punks suspected of robbing the school are swiping much more than easily fenced goods. They are taking away from hundreds of children their best shot at rising above the ghetto: a good education.

"They don't know what they're doing to our education," said Kecia, a tall, skinny sixth grader who weighs 65 pounds and wears her pretty black hair in a braid that circles her head like a garland. "They're just stealing stuff they can sell so they have money in their pocket."

It is easy to break into the school. The west end of the 25-year-old brick building faces a playground and a vacant lot. The windows on that side are waist high. They have been broken so often that they are replaced with Plexiglas or else boarded over.

At 3:30 p.m., the end of the school day, Morgan teachers look like a parade of bag ladies. As a precaution against thieves, the teachers pack their now-precious learning materials and supplies into several shopping bags, tote them out to their cars, and lock the stuff in their car trunks.

Many times, teachers don't have time to clean up the messes left by vandals before the kids arrive for classes at 9:30 a.m.

"Settling the kids after seeing things like that is hard," said Morgan Principal Francis Riley, sixty, a 22-year teaching veteran of Cleveland schools. "There is a degree of fear coping with that. Discipline is affected. . . . Something is happening to our children to make them misbehave all the time. There's so much unlawfulness going on."

Some of Morgan's faculty have taught there for more than twenty years. Back then this Wade Park neighborhood was populated by home owners, mostly black, who looked out for their children's school.

But the 1960s saw the neighborhood slowly slide toward ruin. At the same time, the Cleveland school system declined. It failed to educate its children, and the Cleveland establishment and the news media, cooperating in a conspiracy of silence, did little to let the public know of this shameful situation.

Today the school system does not replace many of the stolen and destroyed items at Morgan Elementary. It doesn't have the money. Morgan doesn't have a refrigerator, ice for bruises or a place for staff lunches. The THINK reading program, which serves 130 sixth graders, was hamstrung for weeks until its cassette recorders were replaced.

And where are the police?

"We rely on police only when something happens," said Riley. "We seldom see police around unless we call. They're here in thirty minutes."

And what of the school district's sound-triggered burglar alarm system provided by Sonitrol Security System Inc. for $250,000 a year?

For whatever reasons, Sonitrol fails 50 percent of the time to notify the Cleveland police and the school security force when break-ins happen at Morgan, Riley says.

"This building has been torn to pieces many times with more than a little noise," said Riley. "I think somebody's sleeping on the job at Sonitrol."

Francis Riley and the Morgan teachers still struggle against these hardships to give their underprivileged pupils a future. It shows. Morgan's standardized test scores in reading and math are near the national average.

And maybe someday Kecia Smith will get the secretary's job she hopes for. Next year, she'll take the bus to Lincoln Junior High School on the West Side.

"I can't wait," she said.

March 29, 1982

Beating the cold

A middle-aged man's voice floated out of the tiny makeshift tent. His words seemed to hang motionless in the heavy frigid air.

"I'm all right," he said. "I've got on five or six pairs of socks. I'm wrapped up in a blanket and a quilt. It's like a sleeping bag. I've got on a couple coats and a couple pairs of pants."

His name is John, and he's one of the scores of homeless men and women wandering the near West Side streets, living from one bottle of wine to the next.

John, fifty-seven, was holed up in his temporary home hidden deep in the brambles that steeply slope from the Riverview housing projects on W. 25th Street down to the Flats.

He had stretched a piece of canvas from a concrete culvert wall to form a lean-to. With cardboard and newspaper he made his tent nearly wind-tight. A blanket of snow covered it all.

On a hanger from a limb hung a bright green sports coat, snow piled on its shoulders like giant epaulets. Three yellow holes in the snow marked John's restroom. From another limb dangled his cupboard, a cardboard box wrapped in plastic.

"I get some food sometimes and put it in there," he said yesterday afternoon. "That keeps it away from the racoons."

Nearly the whole country has been trying to stay warm during this nasty cold spell. Some people use electric blankets, space heaters and hot water bottles. Others down hot toddies and pull on wool socks. Some curl in front of roaring fireplaces, wrapped in afghans. Then there are the freeze babies who insist on taking tropical vacations.

John is a pro at surviving the cold. He was asked to share his tips for staying warm.

"You got to get some plastic," he said from inside his cocoon.

"You can't lie right down on the ground. I've got plastic under here, plywood, a piece of a rug and newspapers."

Why not stay at the City Mission?

"They don't have any room there," he replied. "They only let you stay seven days, maybe ten if it's really cold. There's so many guys out there walking the streets.

"When the weather gets better, I'll do some spot labor," John went on. "I'll make a day's wage, then booze it right up."

Up the hill and a few blocks west of John's nest is a Volunteers of America home for men. It is run by the dedicated Bob and Rebecca Zook.

If you get off the bottle, you can stay there as long as you like. Bob Humphrey, a 51-year-old alcoholic, tried that route a few days ago.

"It's hard right now," he said in the home's reading room. "There's nowhere to go. Last year, there was some empty houses. They're all tore down."

Humphrey gave his advice on staying warm.

"Get two or three topcoats and try to get in a parked car," he said. "You can't just lie down in the cold; you got to get out of it."

Humphrey, an electrician before drink washed away his talents, has a battered pug face and a toothless grin. He passed on another cold weather tip.

"I'd go to jail just to get out of the cold," he said. "I'd have a bottle, and if I saw any officers I'd stagger around, make like I was really drunk. If you get in the Justice Center, they usually give you a blanket and it's not too bad. None of it's nice, but it's better than freezing."

The Terminal Tower concourse is out of bounds this year. "The security guards kick you out," he said.

Ditto for the Greyhound bus terminal. "If the man sees you come in, they ask you to leave," Humphrey said.

Joe Grega sat down at the table after Humphrey left and said: "I'm glad I'm not in Humphrey's condition. He's punch-drunk. I'm a refined wino. I'll be sixty in December."

Grega said he knows how to beat the cold.

"Sleep in basements," he said. "I sleep in basements in the Lakeview projects. There are a lot of locks that are broken over there. I always find a place inside. It's dirty, but it's not cold. It's dangerous: I've had my head beat in many times."

Grega lost his left eye several years ago when two jackrollers stomped his face while he was sleeping it off. One of his drinking buddies fared much worse. He passed out in a truck and froze to death.

"Call it luck," Grega said. "I always find a way out of the cold, even when I'm drinking."

January 18, 1982

Yule war of words

Travel the sidewalk in front of May Company downtown. You're at the nerve center of Christmas foot traffic.

Hear the clamor: buses roaring down Euclid Avenue; heavy machinery rumbling on the Sohio construction site; the cacophony of shoppers' voices; the ding-danging cowbells of charity pitchmen.

Swaddling the din are the amplified voices of two men seeking money: one for the Salvation Army, one for the Volunteers of America. Filter their pleas from their distorted sound systems and you can hear a war of words.

Sherman Porter, a stocky man in a maroon-and-blue Salvation Army cap, was trying yesterday to work the briskly moving lunch crowd. He wanted them to drop money into the bright red kettle in front of Salvation Army's red hut, resting on the sidewalk.

Porter, thirty-three, nestled a microphone stand next to his body and cupped the mike to his mouth. Rocking on his heels, he recited in measured tones:

"I ask you. I beg of you, reach out. This is a special time of the year, my friend. Try to show you love today. Show that you do care today."

Three steps away, the Volunteers of America had set up a collection drum. A man in a Santa Claus suit with a battery powered megaphone and a young guy in a hardhat were making a pitch.

"Nickels, dimes and quarters, that's all we're asking for," said the Volunteers' Santa, his words crackling through the blue-and-white megaphone with its volume setting turned up to nine.

"Nickels, dime and quarters," he repeated, catching a young woman's eye. "Right here, baby. Don't pass it up today." She smiled and kept going.

Porter, the Salvation Army guy, began to talk to a man observing the scene.

"I be on the mike everyday," explained Porter. He nodded to his competitor in the Santa suit. "My personal view is he doesn't know how to talk.

"They claim I be low-rating them for what they are. No way. They be low-rating us. They be messing with us. When they get money, they hold it up and look over at us and be laughing, trying to get me upset so I can't use the mike.

"I think the issue is the way I talk. I draw people. When I leave everyday, he gives me the finger, the guy in the hardhat. My understanding is, we have a conflict every year."

The guy in the Santa suit said his name was Arthur Price. His son, Arthur Price Jr., twenty-eight, was clanging a cowbell and wearing a white hardhat.

"I've been out here for eleven years," said Price, fifty-six. "He [Porter] has been razzing us. He's telling people if you want help, you can't go to us.

"He came over to us at the end of one day and said this is what he thought of the Volunteers of America." To demonstrate, Price the Santa turned his back to the sidewalk crowd, extended his middle finger and bent his elbow in a private, vulgar gesture.

Competition at charity's downtown sweet spot gets enthusiastic. But then, the mostly friendly rivalry between the Salvation Army and Volunteers of America dates back to 1896.

That year, Ballington Booth, head of the Salvation Army in the United States, split from the world organization that was based in London and headed by his father, William Booth. The old man didn't like the way his son ran the U.S. organization along less autocratic lines, and tried to reassign him.

Ballington rebelled against his dad, and formed an offshoot, the Volunteers of America. The tactic of placing his offices next to Salvation Army outposts began back then.

In Cambridge, Massachusetts, for example, a Salvation Army official told a newspaper the Volunteers "opened a hall right at the back of ours and annoyed us in so many ways and tried to get our open-air [meeting] stopped by the chief of police."

The competitors on yesterday's wind-whipped front lines at May Company didn't know they were carrying on tradition. They were enduring the cold, collecting money for their equally worthy causes.

"I'm out here for a purpose, not decoration," said Porter, standing by the Salvation Army red kettle. "I don't stand out in the cold for my health."

A few feet away stood Price, his nose as white as his big fake Santa's beard.

"I haven't been inside yet," he bragged. "Been out here ten days and haven't been inside once."

He glanced at Porter, who was standing in front of the Salvation Army's portable red hut.

"He goes inside," Price sniffed. "They got a heater in there."

December 8, 1983

2
COPS & ROBBERS

Virtue rewarded

Bob Moczulski was still wearing short pants when he decided he wanted to be a policeman.

He came from an old-fashioned family that talked and cared about such old-fashioned things as right and wrong. Moczulski graduated from John Adams High School in 1964. He worked at a bank for a while.

In 1977, he joined the Cleveland police force. Then he began to learn about the shadings people make between right and wrong.

A few months ago, a man called Moczulski's unlisted number at his Parma home and reached his wife. "Tell your (bleep) husband to watch his back," the guy on the phone threatened.

Another day, she got another call from another guy with essentially the same message. Moczulski believes the calls came from Cleveland policemen.

"I'm not playing the game right," he explained. "I've upset the apple cart."

Moczulski apparently broke some policemen's notions of the rules several months ago. He arrested a man for driving while intoxicated and was approached by the man's lawyer, Thomas Italiano.

Italiano is a former Cleveland prosecutor and a part-time law director in Parma. He knew a game played by policemen and lawyers and wanted to see if Moczulski wanted in.

The game goes like this: when people get arrested for minor infractions, the prosecutors rely heavily on the arresting policemen when deciding whether to accept a plea bargain. For example, for a person arrested the first time for DWI, usually the charges are knocked down to reckless operation or failure to maintain physical control of the car. A lesser charge means lower insurance rates for the menace who gets caught drinking and driving.

As a courtesy, prosecutors usually go along with what the policemen recommend. If the drunk was polite when he was arrested, maybe he'll get a reduced charge. If the guy gave the police a hard time, he'll get stuck with DWI.

To those who play the game, money is better than manners. Cash is the trump card.

Italiano tried to bribe Moczulski and his partner, William Hyland, with $50 each. In exchange, they were to agree with whatever reduced charge Italiano worked out with the prosecutor.

Italiano, a lawyer for three decades, got stung. Moczulski guessed what was coming and didn't want to play along. He went to his higher-ups, and they decided to wire him and Hyland with hidden recorders.

The two Second District policemen met separately with Italiano, and he gave them cash.

Italiano was arrested, tried and found guilty of two counts of bribery. Earlier this week, he received a suspended sentence. He stands to lose his license to practice law.

And everyone thinks Moczulski is a hero for nailing a crooked lawyer, right? Not so fast.

Moczulski, who has only five years on the job, found out that his bust of the well-connected lawyer created a firestorm. Some of his police friends had warned him about it.

"They said: 'You're crazy, you're nuts. Do you realize all the crap you're going to get out of this?' " Moczulski recalled.

But he went ahead anyway.

The night Italiano was indicted, someone fired a shot through Moczulski's living room window. He and his wife and two children had been living in Parma for several years without incident. The indictment-night gunshot seemed more than coincidence.

"I've upset the apple cart," Moczulski explained later. "Somebody isn't going to be making his fifty or a hundred bucks a case. I'm taking money out of someone's pocket."

The rules of the game were pointed out to Moczulski once again when some of the old hands in the Second District started giving him the silent treatment.

"After the Italiano thing, some younger policemen, mostly older policemen, won't talk to me at all," Moczulski said. "But that doesn't bother me. I don't care what these guys say. I don't care whether they like me or not. I got enough other policemen, and they're in the majority, who think what I did was right."

The night after Italiano was found guilty, Moczulski wrote a letter about the trial to his parents who live out of town.

"I told them I was thankful that I had them as parents and that they brought me up the way they did," he said.

August 11, 1983

A policeman's lot

The traffic light at E. 9th Street and Carnegie Avenue said, "No Left Turn," and I was late. No traffic cop is going to chase me on the freeway during rush hour, I thought.

Ignoring the sign, I swung onto Interstate 90 and floored the car. In two minutes, a black-and-white cruiser, red light flashing, pulled me over. Despite my excuses and arguments, Patrolman Ronald Tomasch began to write out a ticket.

"You heard of Jimmy Simone, the No. 1 cop?" Tomasch asked. "Well, I'm No. 2 behind him in arrests. I need every one I can get."

Beautiful. Nabbed by a cop spouting an Avis slogan. Just who is this Simone who inspires such competition?

It's a familiar routine. James Simone, thirty-four, climbs into his crisp blue uniform, slips a short-barreled Smith & Wesson in his waistband, pulls on a short black leather jacket and walks a block from his apartment to Second District headquarters on Fulton Road. There he can expect some friendly razzing from the cops.

"It's Supercop."

"Lookit, T.J. Simone."

"Hey, top cop in the West."

Last Sunday, Jimmy Simone marked his tenth year as a Cleveland policeman.

"I look at my work with a lot of pride," said Simone. "I enjoy what I do. You stay at it long enough, you get certain recognition."

Recognition, indeed. Patrolman of the Year in 1980. Valor Award from the Ohio Union of Patrolmen in 1981. Rotary Club's gold medal for heroism in 1981.

Last year wasn't so bad, either. His commander nominated Simone for 1982 Patrolman of the Year. Simone was at or near the top again in various arrest categories: 118 felony; 374 misdemeanor; 1,084 moving violation; 586 parking; 1,281 radio assignments handled.

Simone said he makes a lot of arrests because he lives in the Second District, has worked it for ten years and knows every street character by name.

Another reason: He is an aggressive, gung-ho cop, a workaholic, a man seemingly obsessed with being a success.

"I'm not worried primarily about my safety," he said. "I'm worried more about not being successful. I love police work. That's what I do best in life."

The Second District is Simone's universe. It is bounded by the Cuyahoga River on the east, W. 65th Street on the west, Brookpark Road on the south and Lake Erie on the north.

The Second District is a melting pot. It encompasses the W. 25th Street housing projects, the city's Hispanic community, transplanted Appalachians and the middle-class homeowners south of Cleveland Metroparks Zoo.

Simone and his partners, Alvin Scott and William Wagner, are the Clark Avenue caretakers. They patrol Zone 214: Clark from Scranton Road to W. 65th and environs.

Simone grew up around E. 76th Street and Superior Avenue, a rough ethnic neighborhood where, he said, kids had three career choices: the police department, the priesthood or the penitentiary.

Simone, one of two sons, sang in the choir and served mass. In his early teens, he decided to be a policeman.

By then, his family had moved to Lakewood. He graduated from Lakewood High School in 1966 and enlisted in the Army. He was a paratrooper in Vietnam, making an extra $55 a month for hazardous duty. He earned it.

One time, shrapnel tore into Simone's back, nearly missing his spine. Another time, he and three soldiers were sacked by a grenade. The three others died.

Grenade fragments tore into Simone's carotid artery and jugular vein. He jammed a finger in the hole in his neck and partly stemmed the flow of blood. That move saved his life.

In his ten years on Cleveland's streets, Simone has fared better than in his thirteen months in Vietnam. He's been shot at a dozen times without being hit. He's been in ten shootings, wounding seven men. He has killed two.

"In every case, there was no alternative," Simone said. "One of us was going to die. I love my job. I have three children to support. I intend to come home every night. In those situations where one of us is going to die, I'll be damned if it's going to be me.

"If you go go go 100 percent when you're out there, sooner or later you're going to arrive at a situation where the guy will not give up. And that's what happens. Look at all the situations where I arrived and the guy was still armed and there was no deadly force used by me or my partners, and he was still apprehended."

Several months ago, Simone and his partners, all younger men, were arresting a man at his mother's home. As they struggled to subdue him, the mother pulled a gun and fired at Simone.

He felt the muzzle blast sear his face. A near miss. He and the other cops drew their weapons. "Drop the gun!" Simone yelled.

"We could have killed her on the spot," Simone said later. "She fired at me. [Instead] we disarmed her. See that kind of thing? If I had shot that woman it would have been a front-page story. We were able to take her without shooting her, which is what we are getting paid to do."

A cop is not only a poker-faced enforcer, but is often times a confessor, psychologist and nurse as well.

One night Simone and his partner sped off to a domestic disturbance at a W. 25th Street house where a man lived on the second floor, his girlfriend on the third, and his wife on the first.

They were arguing over where he would sleep that night.

Simone ordered the guy to sleep with the girlfriend on Monday, Wednesday and Friday, and with his wife on Tuesday, Thursday and Saturday. On Sunday, Simone told them, flip a coin.

"I got out of the house and couldn't believe what I had done," he said. "But I'm not supposed to put my values on anybody. Just settle the fights."

Cleveland street patrolmen spend much of their time with the unfortunates barely hanging on to the bottom rung of the social ladder. Many crime victims are just as poor, ignorant and criminal as the perpetrators, studies show.

"Police work in general is like working in a sewer," Simone said. "The hardest thing about the job is not to think like a rat after a while."

Television gives the public a romantic view of police work, Simone believes. It's not the neat, clean world of *CHiPs* or *Adam-12*.

"These guys die with so much class on TV," he said. "On the street, you die a painful, agonizing death. TV doesn't show the blood blowing up against the wall or the guy's head coming off or the eyeballs hanging out."

The stress can be crippling. Last year, two cops in the Second District — they were partners — separately committed suicide. One was near retirement; the other was in his twenties.

In the cop business, the numbers of suicides, broken marriages and careers wrecked by booze are staggering. The figures stack up to ten or more times the national average.

Simone teaches at the Cleveland Police Academy about making arrests. And he counsels policemen involved in shootings.

"It's a very traumatic experience," Simone said. "People don't realize the agony the average policeman goes through. There's always the second-guessing.

"Every confrontation that ended up in a shooting, there was no time to think. It was draw and shoot and hope to God when the smoke cleared you weren't shot or dead. Immediately after the shooting, there's that disbelief that someone tried to kill me. Right after that comes the 'Jesus, I have to justify what I've done.'

"These shootings are all over in a matter of seconds. Then there's the hours of reports, the hours of questioning by homicide and shooting teams. People don't believe you get afraid out there. Then you must live with what happened. The front page article in the paper naming you as the killer of John Doe. They always recount the other shootings you were involved with. You must contend with the accusations of the family.

"People don't realize, probably because of TV policemen, that at night, in an alley, in a situation where you have to use your firearm, you can't shoot a gun out of a guy's hand. You shoot with the idea of protecting yourself or your partner or someone else.

"I could never tell you in advance when the bullet's gonna strike. I'm not sure the bullet's going to hit him. Most of the time I shoot out of blind fear. When it's over with, someone's down."

Policemen deal with stress in ways as different as their personalities. Many come down off the adrenaline high of a dangerous day by drinking at the various cop bars around town.

Others, like Simone, turn to exercise. Simone, who rarely drinks, is 5-feet-8 and weighs 160 to 165 pounds. At the end of a shift, he may put on his running shoes and burn off tension running two miles through his neighborhood.

At home, some simple domestic chores put him at ease: tending his plants and his garden.

"This is my sanctuary," Simone said, waving his hand around his nicely furnished apartment. "My home time is my real enjoyment."

Police work — with its rotating shifts, missed holidays with the family, nagging tensions — helped snuff his former marriage. He was a well-paid phone installer for Ohio Bell Telephone Company right before going into the police academy, and his family was used to his regular hours.

Now, Simone lives with Lynne Stachowiak, twenty-three, a police dispatcher for the Sixth District. She works the same hours and shifts he does, and knows well the peculiarities of police work.

"We get along great," she said. "Maybe because we work the same kind of job, the same hours, and we spend all our time together. We have a very level, stable relationship."

February 27, 1983

Concealed weapon

She fell in love with an aggressive street cop. Now she lives with a burden: he could be killed at any time.

Lynne Stachowiak, twenty-four, has been with detective Jimmy Simone, thirty-five, less than two years, but she knows his story: a paratrooper in 'Nam who caught shrapnel in his neck, a veteran of ten shootings during his eleven years on the police force.

Lynne understands policemen better than most. She's a police dispatcher. She relays calls to the black-and-whites, sending them into life-threatening situations.

She understands, which explains why she worries. For instance, last Christmas she gave Jimmy a gold chain with a medal blessed by the police chaplain. On the back of the medal, she had engraved the letters, "A.T.C." Always take care.

Jimmy never takes off the medal.

Lynne was working last Wednesday morning when another dispatcher sent Second District police on a hot run: A man had stolen a car at gunpoint, dumped it and fled into a West Side church. Police began a search of the building.

Soon the radio air was crackling. "We got two men down."

A few minutes later, a report made Lynne jump: A plainclothes cop had been shot. She just knew it was Jimmy. A co-worker confirmed it and Lynne left work.

She ran into the hospital. Standing around were about a dozen cops from Simone's platoon.

They are a tight-knit platoon nicknamed the Headhunters because they make more arrests and respond more quickly than any other of the city's eighteen platoons.

The Headhunters were all crying. Three of their buddies were down.

"Tell me he's not dead!" Lynne begged them.

Simone and Patrolmen John J. Thomas, twenty-eight, and Brian Miller, twenty-four, lay in the emergency room hooked to blood bags and intravenous gear.

She pulled her face down to Jimmy's and he said softly: "I'm gonna be all right. I'm sorry, there was no other way."

The bullet had entered his left cheek and exited behind his ear. An inch in either direction and his brains would have been on the church floor.

Gradually, the story was pieced together for her: Simone and Thomas and Miller began searching the church basement. Thomas was carrying a shotgun.

Except for a closet, they had finished the search. Simone crouched on one knee, his gun drawn, ready to open the door. Thomas stood a few feet behind with the shotgun, his safety on. Miller stood three feet to his side.

Simone swung the door. Mennis David Workman, thirty-one, jumped out, blasting Simone in the face with a .38 revolver. Workman kept firing, hitting Thomas in the thigh and Miller in the left arm, the one he shoots with.

The first bullet knocked Simone to the floor. Workman sprang back into the closet. The gunman came out again and began firing. Simone, the closest, pulled off five shots.

"They couldn't immediately return fire," Simone would say later. "I was in the way. I was trying to get up and get out of there."

The three wounded policemen took cover behind a four-foot partition and had a conversation.

"Johnny, I'm hit bad," Simone said, bleeding furiously.

"I'm hit," Thomas replied.

"I'm hit too," Miller said.

"I'm going to reload," Simone said. Thomas and Miller laid down a cover of gun fire toward the closet while Simone, his eyes blinded by blood, reloaded by feel and began to pray.

It was agreed that Thomas and Miller should crawl out before they lost too much blood. This time, Simone fired his gun at the closet to cover for them. Then he began to crawl out of the basement. He slipped in a pool of blood, fell on his side, and dropped his gun. He couldn't pick it up. Shock was setting in.

Simone thought, "I'm gonna die."

Lt. Gregory Baeppler, Simone's platoon commander, made it to the bleeding cop as another cop covered with gunfire.

"Tell my kids what happened down here," Simone told him.

"You tell 'em," the lieutenant said. "We're getting out of here."

The suspect, Workman, probably didn't notice the gunfire. He lay on his back in the closet, gushing blood from a hole in his chest.

When emergency room workers cut off Simone's clothes, they removed his medal and put it in an envelope.

Later, one of the policemen brought the medal to Lynne. She wiped off the crusted blood. Always take care.

"I'll have to get it another blessing," she said later. "I think we used that one up."

November 21, 1983

Above the law

You can't tell by looking at them, but there's a special class of citizens in Cleveland.

You can figure out their status by peering into their wallets and purses. Not for the green stuff. For a small blue card they keep next to their driver's license.

It's called a courtesy card; it can keep its owner from getting ticketed for speeding, running stop signs and red lights, maybe even for drunken driving.

Over the years, tens of thousands of these cards have been issued by the Cleveland Police Patrolmen's Association and the Fraternal Order of Police.

Say you make an illegal left turn. A policeman pulls you over and asks for your driver's license. If you're a member of the courtesy club, you whip out your free pass.

Many of the privileged set keep their courtesy cards with their driver's licenses in those see-through plastic covers. No wasted motion.

Unless you mouth off, brandish a gun, or offer him a sniff of your stash, the patrolman will almost certainly let you go without a ticket.

If you're pals with a policeman, you already know about the wonderful convenience of courtesy cards. It's been going on for decades.

If the arrangement seems like a double standard of justice, you're right.

I asked a policeman in the Third District if he honored courtesy cards.

"Sure," he said.

What are they good for?

"Any traffic stuff."

How about a DWI?

"I let a couple of people go. They were sleeping in their van. They pulled out all kinds of cards and we let 'em go."

Since when is sleeping a crime?

"It was broad daylight. In the middle of an intersection. At a green light. I guess he stopped for a breather. Turned out to be an hour and a half nap."

By the way, each card is numbered and carries the name of the policeman who issued it.

The Third District man I talked to said he told the drunk's friend on the police force about the incident. He in turn called the drunk and said, "Those two guys did you a favor."

So the drunk gave the two policemen a present. Guess what?

"We ended up with a couple of bottles of whiskey," the Third District man said.

But the guy in the van was smashed. What about public safety?

"You're passed out in a car and you find a policeman knocking on the window — that can sober you up fast," the policeman reasoned.

A detective in the Fourth District remembers busting a young woman for selling drugs. From her purse, she pulled three blue courtesy cards.

"Do these help?" she asked.

"No," the detective laughed. "They don't help."

Safety Director Reginald Turner doesn't want police to honor courtesy cards. He thinks it looks bad. Further, courtesy cards basically transfer power and discretion from management into the hands of individual policemen.

"I believe it's inappropriate," Turner said. "It has no standing in law. It's not sanctioned by me."

But there's nothing he's going to do about it.

Police Chief William Hanton said courtesy cards should not influence policemen's decisions. But it's unlikely Hanton will buck the courtesy system.

William McNea, president of the patrolmen's union, thinks courtesy cards are dandy.

"We think they're good public relations," he said. "It's a courtesy that says you're a friend of a policeman."

He added: "They're not a passport to sin."

Every year, each Cleveland patrolman whose dues are paid up gets a set of courtesy cards to spread around. McNea guesses there are 20,000 cards in the Cleveland area, probably a low estimate.

"They can get as many as they ask for," McNea said.

I asked McNea why not call a moratorium on courtesy cards? Think of all the extra $50 traffic tickets police could issue. With that extra money, maybe the city could put some of the laid-off policemen back to work?

McNea acted like he was asked to shoot the family pet.

"Why zero in on us?" he said. "The city should be going after parking tickets already issued."

Right. And the city better hurry up. In the meantime, police just might come up with a courtesy card that wipes out the overdue parking tickets.

May 31, 1984

The comedy beat

He was a Cleveland cop moonlighting as a security guard at the Cleveland Comedy Club. For months he sat there in his blue uniform, his eyes on the lookout for rowdies, his ears tuned to the parade of polished pros and amateurish locals working the crowds for laughs.

One day, Tom Alusheff told himself, "I can do that."

He made his move on a Sunday — Amateur Night — when anyone with the nerve can commandeer a microphone and run his schtick by the audience. Fueled with eight Molsons, clutching a list of 12 jokes, Alusheff strode into the spotlight on the tiny stage.

No monologue, no impressions, no sight gags; just a string of jokes without transitions. Surprisingly, he knocked 'em dead. The crowd laughed so hard the burly cop was embarrassed. Alusheff won $50, and a rising star was born.

"They were old locker-room jokes," the patrolman recalled. "Nothing original. I was always good at telling jokes. I can remember jokes I heard five, eight years ago and tell them exactly. I got a good memory."

Alusheff, twenty-nine, adopted the stage name "Morey Cohen," a tip of the hat to Myron Cohen, the old master of Yiddish humor. In the last year, when he hasn't been in a zone car in the Third District or spending time with his new wife, Mary, Alusheff-Cohen has been working nightclubs in Columbus, Fort Lauderdale and Toronto, as well as the Comedy Club, the Ground Floor Restaurant & Lounge and fund-raisers and parties around town.

Alusheff grew up in Collinwood. His grandparents came from Macedonia, a disputed region in Greece and Yugoslavia. His father is Chris Alusheff, owner of Baker Candies, home of the famous chocolate-covered whipped cream eggs.

When he was a child, Tom wrote a letter to former Clevelander Bob Hope. "Dear Bob Hope," the letter read. "I want to be a comedian when I grow up. How do I do it?"

A few weeks later, he got his reply: an autographed picture of Hope. Tommy took it to show-and-tell at Nottingham School.

Before working as a policeman, Alusheff was a state park ranger, a bouncer at the Agora nightclub and a security guard at Margaret Spellacy Junior High in Collinwood.

Now he's the dark-haired guy with the gruff voice who patrols the downtown and near East Side streets.

He doesn't work police jokes into his routine. In fact, he uses comedy as an escape from the ulcerous brew of boredom, high speed, humor and occasional violence that makes up patrol car work.

"A zone car man is like a floor-sweeper," Alusheff said. "The only place you can go is up. I'd like better hours, maybe get into a detective bureau. I know I can be more useful outside of a zone car. I speak three languages: English, Serbo-Croatian and Macedonian. . . .

"It got to the point where I was expected to tell a joke at roll call every day," continued the comic cop. "The sergeant would say: 'Any words of wisdom, Morey?' I always got everybody laughing with whatever joke popped in my mind."

Like what?

He told a joke. Sorry, it won't clean up for family reading.

"Policemen have a pretty morbid sense of humor," he allowed.

Alusheff can't always escape police work while working as a comic. He tells a funny story about that.

"Like I was saying, I found a way to get out of my uniform and make some part-time money without being a cop," he began. "So I'm doing a show at Case Western, a fraternity night. There was a gambling area and a bar. Comedians went up between bands. No bouncers there at all.

"Case owns Ohio Diesel Tech, one of those piston-head schools. You got these grease monkeys who go to this school and live down at Case with the Ivy League kids. I hear they just terrorize them down there.

"Anyway, the motor heads are inside this bar. It surprised me they didn't have any security at all. I was onstage and saw a fight break out in back. I thought it was a joke. I said: 'Hit 'em, smack 'em, hit 'em for me.' All of a sudden a buddy's wife runs up: 'Tommy, Tommy, they're beating up Jerry' — another comic.

"I pull one guy off, I get Jerry out of there. These guys start again, picking on people randomly. We broke it up again. I grab a bartender and tell him to call University Circle police. They come, I identify myself and say: 'These two guys gotta go.'

"They haul them to the Fifth District and I book 'em for DCI [disorderly conduct, intoxicated]. You never make an off-duty DCI. You just don't do that off-duty. There I am trying to get away from my job, and I have to arrest two guys."

A typical Cleveland gig for Morey Cohen might start out: "Anybody here from Collinwood? Hey, put the gun down, pal. You know Collinwood, the East Side neighborhood where they tore down buildings to build slums. . . .

"It was tough growing up in Collinwood. For instance, in kindergarten we had that federal breakfast program: bowl of cereal, glass of juice and a Thorazine tablet . . . . I'm Macedonian. I tell people that and they say: 'Hey, I got an aunt in Twinsburg.' "

Alushuff likes comedy and police work for the same reason.

"It's tied in with being a cop, wanting to help people and all that stuff," he said. "I really feel good making all those people laugh out there. I can't believe I could go up there for ten minutes, make people roar, and get paid for it. I make fifty bucks for ten minutes. It would take me five hours in uniform in a bank parking lot to make fifty bucks.

"It [comedy] is the same as catching a burglar in a house, doing the paper work and not having to go to court because he pleads guilty. You get a good feeling."

Alusheff would like to make it big.

"It's always in the back of my head," he admitted. "But it's just too much to lose, to leave my job and kick and claw in that business. It's a cut-throat business. You pay your dues in Cleveland, you still got to scrape for two years to get your chance on Letterman or Carson.

"If I made $100,000 a year, sure, I'd drop the police department in a minute. But maybe you can make $100,000 for a couple years, and then you're never heard from again."

September 15, 1983

That kitten case

It was a warm summer night and Sgt. Peter Gawry moved with deliberation. He picked up his 12-gauge shotgun loaded with birdshot, went outside and looked for the kitten hanging around the Middleburg Heights police station.

Patrolmen had been feeding the new stray, as they had with other strays. One officer had planned to take the kitten home that night.

Gawry saw the kitten, aimed his shotgun and fired. Blam!

The gray fluffy carcass, its intestines spilling out, lay on the sidewalk. Soon, news spread across the country about a lawman who killed a police-station pet.

Sgt. Gawry, forty-one, has never been married. He is a 15-year veteran and the number three man on the force. He is a complicated cop. One day he instructs his men in firearm safety. Another day he supposedly pulls his gun, waves it around and points it at city workers.

Middleburg Heights police regulations say an animal can be shot only if it's dangerous or severely injured. Was the kitten a public menace?

Police Chief Robert Blatnica answered the question: "I don't know if it was. . . . The rules stipulate you use reasonable measures unless it's vicious or attacks you."

Was the kitten vicious? Did it attack Gawry?

"I don't think it was vicious," the chief said. "He [Gawry] was going along the lines it was a stray, half-starved, and [he was] fearful it would get under a car."

But the cat was being fed by patrolmen for a week. If it were half-starved, why didn't Gawry act earlier?

"I don't know," the chief replied. "He didn't use good judgment.

If the cat were sick, like [Gawry] said it was, then there were other ways to handle it. He could have turned it over to the animal warden."

Yesterday, Blatnica suspended Gawry for thirty days without pay and ordered him to pass physical and psychiatric tests before returning to duty.

A Middleburg Heights policeman detailed how Gawry executed the kitten: Gawry was told that another policeman was going to take the kitten home that night to join the three other strays he had picked up at the station. Gawry then picked up his gun, went outside and fired at the stray.

His actions upset some policemen, but apparently didn't shock them. They said they're used to such actions by now.

Two members of the police force and another city worker contend that Gawry has pulled his gun on them and said something like: "I got the drop on you. I could have shot you."

Was he joking? one policeman was asked.

"It didn't seem like it," the cop retorted. "I wouldn't tolerate that joke from a friend of mine."

Another city worker said Gawry, while on duty several years ago, pulled his service revolver and pointed it at him.

"That's the only time he did it," the worker said. "Pete's been a friend. I don't like people pulling a gun on me, joking or not. I told him how I felt."

Said another cop who claimed he ended up on the wrong end of Gawry's gun: "He's a cowboy. I can't think of a day he hasn't had his gun out, waving it around. It's a macho thing for him."

The police chief denies ever seeing Gawry wave his gun. The chief said he's heard the stories, but hasn't asked Gawry about them yet.

A lot of residents of Middleburg Heights know Pete Gawry. They say he's a good guy. Which he probably is — most of the time.

Why should he lose his job over a stray cat, friends ask. After all, thousands of cats are put to sleep each day by animal wardens across the country. What's the big deal about the death of a stray that just eats and eliminates?

Here's the big deal. This guy blasted his shotgun in a parking lot and debris from the shot supposedly bounced up and hit a woman, who luckily was not injured. Gawry's act was cruelty to an animal. He is a law enforcer who carries a gun and is supposed to protect us and he acts erratically.

Police forces across the country have a dark secret. Some of their law enforcers are no longer temperamentally suited for the job. The stress has gotten to them. They've begun to unravel.

"There's a lot of stress," Chief Blatnica admitted. "We just got over that hot-rod show. There were four thousand people at Bagley and Engle [Roads]. Add a little booze to that situation — it was rough."

All kinds of professionals unravel under stress: lawyers, medics, politicians, principals, reporters. None of them carries a gun.

Maybe it's a good thing Gawry killed that kitten and got attention focused on him. It could have been a lot worse.

July 14, 1983

Tell no lies to Sgt. Kovacic

It's 7:30 p.m., time for "Lie Detector." Cameras cut to the pugnacious, squinting face of lawyer F. Lee Bailey. A deep-voiced announcer intones: "F. Lee Bailey, he goes anywhere to find the truth." Viewers then are treated to a montage of Bailey's more famous cases, and the anonymous voice sums it up: " 'Lie Detector,' the show that gets to the truth."

The truth about lie detector tests?

"Twentieth-century witchcraft," thunders former senator Sam Ervin Jr.

"An effective, reliable tool," insists Lynn Marcy, president of the American Polygraph Association.

"No one can beat the test," boasts Bailey.

"An invasion of privacy," complains the American Civil Liberties Union.

Sgt. Victor Kovacic of the Cleveland Police Department has an opinion about the polygraph.

Kovacic has administered thousands of tests, extracting confessions from the guilty and freeing the innocent. He holds Patent No. 3977393 on a blood-pressure cuff, now used with most new polygraphs. Occasionally, a royalty check finds its way to his mailbox.

Kovacic's opinion: "It's strictly an investigative aid and a truth verifier."

Kovacic is head of the police Scientific Investigation Unit. He's tall and strong-jawed, sort of a young-looking Robert Stack.

He oversees the work of fifty people who trace weapons, examine evidence at crime scenes, analyze drugs, x-ray suspected bombs, dismantle bombs, identify guns, maintain fingerprint files and give hundreds of polygraph exams.

Kovacic spent last week on a backhoe, digging up the ground in the Wildwood Park area in search of twenty ounces of nitroglycerine.

"Polygraphs probably started out being controversial," he explained, "because people had interpreted the polygraph as being the last word and authority, usurping the prerogative of the jury."

Adding to the controversy are the incompetent private examiners working Kovacic's turf. Ohio is one of ten states that do not license polygraph examiners. We've got our share of fly-by-nights.

"It's a dangerous tool if there aren't controls," Kovacic acknowledged. "The accuracy of the lie test depends on the competency of the examiner."

Indeed, as lawsuits filed in Common Pleas Court indicate, jobs are lost and reputations destroyed by unqualified examiners.

Bailey prepares John, a Yonkers, N.Y., house painter, for the lie test. John is accused of stealing two rings on the job. John sits strapped in a chair. Wires are hooked to his fingertips. His shiny forehead looks pasty compared to Bailey, the ruddy host.

An element of suspense is introduced: If John passes the test, he gets his job back from Mr. Whelan, his boss. We must decide whom to root for: the contraption or the sweaty house painter.

Cameras cut to four giant graphs. They are labeled, "upper breathing," "lower breathing," "G.S.R." [galvanic skin response] and "blood pressure." Over the sound track, a simulated heartbeat is pounding like a tom-tom drum. Four stylus arms scratch up and down on the graph paper as John answers the question.

THUMP thump THUMP thump THUMP thump goes the soundtrack.

"This is the control question," Bailey informs us in a conspiratorial whisper. "He shouldn't be worried about it unless he stole those rings."

THUMP thump THUMP thump THUMP thump.

"We have freed a lot of persons who were wrongfully accused," Kovacic said, recalling one case:

Two innocent men were found guilty of murdering Kenneth R. Houser, an off-duty Cleveland policeman, at Cliff's Bar on Buckeye Road on April 2, 1969. Michael P. Jones and Allen Pinkney, the wrongfully imprisoned men, spent more than a year in the penitentiary.

Then, acting on a tip, police asked a man to take the lie test.

"Based upon interpretations of the charts, I asked him more specifically about the case," Kovacic said. "He confessed to his part and the parts of others. I was able to learn the real person who committed the murder and the background behind it. . . . Ultimately, we put the right people in the pen."

Kovacic and the Ohio Association of Polygraph Examiners have been trying for years to get state legislators to pass a law requiring polygraph examiners to be licensed.

But many unions, notably those representing retail workers, oppose licensing. They believe it would legitimize a dangerous, inaccurate tool. Depending on which study you read, lie tests are 40 percent to 95 percent accurate.

One problem is the dependence of many businesses on the polygraph. Example: Suppose some inventory is missing. A company will force all of its employees to take lie tests to prove their innocence. Critics consider this an invasion of privacy and degrading to workers.

Some Greater Cleveland businesses known to have used lie tests include Friday's restaurants, Radio Shack, J.B. Robinson Jewelers, Cook United Inc., Revco Discount Drug Centers, Sohio and many banks, hotels, retail merchants and small manufacturing companies.

"I see it as a valuable investigative tool for businesses and all industries," Kovacic said. "If you have a rotten apple in a bushel, it becomes necessary to examine all of them to find the one that is rotten."

Kovacic, forty-nine, is a 22-year veteran of the Cleveland Police Department. His two cousins are also city policemen. Kovacic grew up around E. 61st Street and St. Clair Avenue. He was a standout athlete at East High School, was signed by the Cleveland Indians and spent some time pitching in the minor leagues. He had a big fastball, but lacked big-league control.

After a few months as a patrolman in a zone car, Kovacic joined the crime lab. He learned it all: ballistics identification, fingerprinting, polygraphs. He knows all about polygraph exams, but "I don't think I could beat it" if the lie test were administered by a competent examiner, he said.

"There is one way to beat it," he likes to say. "Don't take the test at all."

Kovacic thinks polygraph results should be admissible in court. After all, eyewitness testimony — the weakest, most error-prone form of evidence — is allowed in the courtroom. Polygraph supporters say the tests are much more reliable than somebody's memory.

Kovacic is less than enthusiastic about Bailey's legal Gong Show. He's never seen "Lie Detector," which has dealt with such weighty issues as whether a pro wrestler faked a match and whether Zsa Zsa Gabor married for money. But he has an opinion.

"A TV studio would be a very poor place to conduct a proper polygraph exam," Kovacic said charitably.

Bailey grabs the four charts from his examiner and pulls sweaty John into camera range. The lawyer begins his post-game analysis.

"Take a good look at these charts," he tells John, who looks bewildered. "I hate to tell you this, John, but this is a record on our show. You have registered minus 41 in deception."

The camera hangs on John's pasty face, waiting for a reaction. John merely stares woodenly.

Bailey works him for a confession: "C'mon, John, why did you come on the show? What did you want to tell us? How can you explain these charts?"

"I don't know," says John. "I just don't know. I can't believe it."

Time is running out. Bailey looks at John and says it looks like he won't be getting his job back.

"I'm sorry, John," Bailey says with the slightest smirk. "I'm going to have to tell Mr. Whelan no dice."

April 10, 1983

A civil service

The vilest deeds, like poison weeds,
bloom well in prison air.
It's only what's good in man
that wastes and withers there.

— Oscar Wilde

Today, a state civil service team descends on the county jail to examine the job of corrections officer. The team is supposed to create a test that jailers will have to pass before being hired.

Some hope the test will weed out nitwits.

Testing potential jailers, which will start in about a year, will be a big change. Presently, corrections officers don't have to have grade school educations or clean criminal records.

"Yeah, we got some [bleep]ing jerks," Cuyahoga County Sheriff Gerald T. McFaul acknowledged. "I had a guy who couldn't write his name. But I knew it when I hired him. He was alert, not some guy who went, 'duh, duh, duh.' We put him in sanitation. He scrubbed floors. He worked six months, quit and went back to West Virginia."

Then there was the card-playing jailer who lost a bet with inmates and had to perform push-ups as a payoff. As the guy went up and down, three inmates under his care punched out a window, slipped down the jail tower and escaped for several hours.

When he heard about the embarrassing escape, McFaul said he "went fruitcake."

"Ninety-eight percent of our corrections officers are decent, sincere young guys," he said. "Some of 'em don't give a damn. They're only here because they can't find a job. They admit it. See, when they come in here, they're like little altar boys. They're on probation for four months. But soon after sixteen weeks, they tell everybody to go [bleep] themselves. Because now they're civil service employees.

"And they don't even take civil service tests. That's what [bleep]s me off."

Tom Kemmett, a burly guy at 6-feet-4, has worked for five years as a corrections officer. One of 371 corrections officers, Kemmett will be making the top salary next year, $18,500.

"I have what you call a thankless job," he explained. "I work six days a week with no overtime. I work all the holidays that fall on my six days, with no overtime. 'Course, I get time coming, but I have to put in for the day with a seven day notice and a reason why I want the day off.

"I work in a place where there is nothing but hatred and tension. I work for a boss who makes me feel worthless. If you work long enough, you begin to doubt your own worth.

"I work in an area known as a pod," Kemmett went on. "This pod contains twenty-two or twenty-three inmates on the tenth floor, the maximum-security floor. There're eight pods on the tenth floor, and there's supposed to be nine COs working the floor. But most of the time we have only five officers. This means I'm supposed to watch two pods, forty-four to forty-six inmates, with no way to get past the staggered gates quickly [if there's trouble], unless the corrections officer across the hall deserts his post to help me out.

"I've had human waste tossed on me. I've been spit on. I have thirty-two stitches in my mouth, and I have cracked teeth. I've been kicked, punched, threatened, and my family's been threatened. My windshield has been broken out. My tires have been flattened.

"I have so many rules that I can't get through a day without breaking any. If I do get caught, let's say that I forgot to punch my time clock, I get a one day suspension.

"When I first started here five years ago, I was sent up into the jail with nothing but my civilian clothes. No training, no nothing. I was handed keys and I was told to watch forty-six inmates and that was my on-the-job training.

"After two years, I received formal training of eighty hours, but it was really sixty.

"My job is the same every day — filled with mind-numbing boredom. Six days of nothing, no hope, no future, no nothing. Day in and day out, you hear the inmates gripe about the medical care, the social workers, the library, the rec, and the food. They only have me to complain to, and I only have my wife.

"Someone may wonder why I stay here. It's because it's a job and someone has to do it. Also, because I have this job, two people are still alive. I saved two inmates from hanging."

"I wouldn't want to work upstairs," Sheriff McFaul was saying. "Psychologically, you're a prisoner. When you punch that time clock, you're confined in that cell block for eight hours. You eat the same goddam food, you drink the same coffee, you rap the same [bleep], you're one of them."

Will a civil service test bring better jailers and a safer jail?

"You could take the test and pass with flying colors and you could be the poorest employee I got," McFaul replied. "Maybe you can't stomach the job. The best employees I got are the street guys. They come in and check in and say: 'Howya doin', my man.'

"I get some young kid from Parma — his father calls me and says he's a nice kid, big, 6-feet-2. He's scared. He's never dealt with minorities. The best employees I got are the street guys. Real tough SOBs from the street. Nobody [bleep]s with 'em."

October 24, 1983

3

LOVERS & FIGHTERS

A West Side story

It was 1966 and we were easy to spot. Thick algebra books, short hair and neckties marked us as freshmen at St. Ignatius High School.

We were mostly middle-class kids from the suburbs who carried pocket money. After classes or practice, we'd cut down Lorain Avenue or the sidestreets to W. 25th Street and catch a bus or rapid home.

In the nearby Riverview projects, Joe D'Angelo and his buddies were poor, inner-city whites, blacks and Puerto Ricans. They cut classes, fought when they attended school and hustled to get spending money.

One hustle was jumping the Ignatius kids.

"They had money, I didn't, and I took it from them," Joe recalled the other day. "We used to walk over to the rapid transit and wait for them. It's not something I'm proud of. You kids had more money, and if you lost a couple bucks, it was no big deal."

The near West Side was rough. Ohio City's turn-of-the-century houses had not yet been dolled up. Heck's was a lunch counter selling greasy hamburgers for thirty cents. Every block seemed to have a flop house or a dope house or a bust-out bar.

There were loose-knit gangs at the projects, falling mainly along ethnic lines. Joe was a big kid and not afraid to fight. But he didn't get involved in the gangs and their heavy action. He watched from the sidelines.

"Peer pressure," he said, explaining why he helped shake down the Ignatius kids. "You were worried about being tough."

He's a bear of a guy at six feet, 230 pounds. With a bushy beard and graying hair, he looks like a young Kenny Rogers.

Today, Joe is thirty-two and married. He has two kids, three houses, an Old Brooklyn bar and a dream: to retire at forty-five. Last night at a big hotel he attended one of those upbeat, inspirational seminars telling you how to make a fortune in real estate.

"In order to be able to have something," Joe explained, "you got to work for it."

Joe's West Side story shows that you can start out poor and uneducated, and still pull yourself up by the bootstraps.

He grew up around E. 93rd Street and Miles Avenue. His father, an alcoholic, abandoned him and his two sisters and his mother for a while. When he returned, the family had moved into the subsidized projects on W. 25th Street. Joe was ten. Six years later, his dad had drunk himself to death and Joe had quit school for good.

"I went through the phase of fighting, carrying on, drugs," he said. "A lot of people I've grown up with are still stuck in that particular phase. Their life circulates around drugs, no job. They have enough money to go from day to day, waiting for their welfare checks. I just don't want that kind of stuff."

Joe worked. First as a cook at Arnold's Restaurant on W. 65th Street. Then he talked his way into a job at a plumbing company and mastered the trade after several years. He quit for more money as a plumber at St. Alexis Hospital.

Along the way, Joe did outside plumbing jobs, tended bar at the Dry Dock and other places, and saved money.

"Anytime you could hustle, I was hustling," he said. "I always wanted better."

In 1978, he looked around and found a failing bar on State Road in Old Brooklyn. Joe bought it, put in a color TV, a stove and a microwave oven for selling sandwiches.

It's a typical blue-collar, neighborhood bar with a pool table and a jukebox. Joe sells mixed drinks for eighty-five cents and sponsors a bowling team.

"Now it's a thriving little thing that does fine for me," Joe said. "I try to keep it from being a punch palace."

He bought a home around Fleet Avenue and sends his kids to parochial grade school. With savings, he bought two other modest houses and fixed them up to rent them.

He's still not content. He wants more property, other businesses and financial security.

"I'd like to retire at forty-five and just relax," he said. "Why retire to Florida at sixty-five when you're too old to enjoy it? I'm not a workaholic. Work doesn't make me tick. I really have to get yself motivated in the mornings."

So why strive so hard?

"I want more because of my kids," he said. "I'm not greedy. I st want more. Now my kids say they need $25 for school pic-res or ten for cheerleading, and I've got it. There was none of at when I was growing up.

"Now I'll be in a position to send my kids to Ignatius," he said. hope they don't get jumped."

June 2, 1983

Standing fast

Inez Moore may be an unknown heroine. She may die today or tomorrow or next week from untreatable cancer. But she fought good fight and won. Her accomplishment survives.

Moore was a frail 60-year-old widow living at 1854 Garfiel Road in East Cleveland when she was sentenced to five days in ja and hit with a $25 fine in 1973.

Her crime: She was living with her 10-year-old grandson, John whom Moore took in after his mother died.

Inez Moore was already housing her son, Dale, and his son Dale Jr. She had raised both grandchildren from infancy.

She had been residing in the Central neighborhood until the cit knocked down her home to make way for a school. She moved to East Cleveland in 1970.

An East Cleveland ordinance passed in 1966 defined "family" to exclude John. The law said only "one family" plus one "authorized person" could live under one roof. John, therefore, was an "unli censed boarder" and had to go.

Moore could have acted like so many of her neighbors by selling her house and moving. She refused.

"It was a very terrible situation," Moore said yesterday. "I found that the only way it could be solved was to take it to the courts."

She lost in every court in Ohio that heard her case, and ended up before the U.S. Supreme Court in 1977.

As she sat in the Supreme Court, she scrutinized each justice's expression as Legal Aid Society lawyer Edward R. Stege Jr. argued the case.

"I had it figured out," Moore said. "All but three would be in my favor."

The vote was 5 to 4 in her favor. She misjudged Chief Justice

Warren Burger.

"He had grandchildren, so I thought he'd be understanding," she said.

In his opinion, Justice William Brennan Jr. wrote that the Constitution does not permit "white suburbia's preference" for the nuclear family to be imposed "by government on the rest of us."

Today, Moore is sixty-nine and rests in a hospital bed set on the wood floor of her dining room. Two large bottles of aspirin, a box of tissues and a water glass occupy a night stand.

She is a mere stick figure, carrying sixty-three pounds on her 5-foot-6 frame. Her forearms are thin, square-edged slats.

"Skin and bones," she said. "That's all I am."

Her hands are crabbed; arthritis crippled her fingers years ago. But she still scribbles thank you notes by pinching a pen between her movable thumb and forefinger.

If she hadn't decided to battle the injustice, East Cleveland might be enforcing its anti-family ordinance today. You could only guess how many families would be split up in East Cleveland and hundreds of other cities.

Today's economy has forced sons and daughters to move in with their parents and grandparents just to stretch unemployment checks or meet grocery bills.

"I had plenty of people [back then] tell me they had to move out," Moore said. "The economy is bad today. How can people afford a place to rent when they can live [together] cheaper?"

Inez Moore, by her example, has shown that the work of one person can make a difference. In these times of hardship, when society seems complex and unchangeable, people like Moore are an inspiration. It's often the ordinary folks with heart who improve our lives.

After all, Rosa Parks was only a tired black woman in Montgomery, Alabama, who was ordered by a driver to vacate her seat in the black section of a crowded bus so a white man could sit. She refused and was jailed. Her then-rebellious stand in 1955 catalyzed the emerging civil rights movement.

After all, Lois Gibbs was just an anonymous housewife in the Love Canal section of Niagara Falls who almost never read a newspaper. But she took a stand when she found out that her son and daughter had diseases possibly linked to the tons of toxic chemicals buried in her middle-class neighborhood. She organized a fight that took on President Jimmy Carter, New York's governor and the Environmental Protection Agency. She won.

After all, Oliver Brown was just a black Topeka, Kansas, railroad worker who sued the city Board of Education in 1951 for not allowing his daughter to attend a school near their home that happened to be all-white. Brown took his case to the U.S. Supreme Court. He won. The decision began the end of unequal segregated school systems.

These ordinary folks would understand the convictions of Inez Moore.

"I felt I was right all the way," Moore explained. "That's why I went after it. If I had one doubt, I wouldn't have gone after it. I believe in my convictions. I knew in my heart I was right.

"You have to fight for yourself. No one's gonna fight for you. You can't give up."

March 31, 1983

A tale of two loves

It had been three years since he had heard her voice.

Then last week she called. She called the Cleveland Play House and asked to speak to him.

"We'd like to come to your show," she told him.

We?, Si thought. *We?*

"I owe you $200," she went on. "I'm getting married."

It was a dozen years ago when Silas Osborne and Cassie (not her real name) made a pact. They were sweethearts at Solon High School and agreed that if they didn't marry each other, whoever married first would have to pay the other the then noble sum of $200.

Si sailed off to Rocky Mountain College in Billings, Montana, to study American Indians and to become a social worker on the reservations.

Cassie stayed near home at a small college in Ohio.

Si worked on ranches, took up theater and after three years of college, left Montana to study method acting in New York.

They were long-distance lovers for years. They wrote each other long, frequent letters to keep their romance tight, but Si had become a footloose actor. He lived in Chicago and spent seasons in Cleveland, San Francisco and other cities.

He began to realize that Cassie wanted someone steady and dependable, but he always wrote, always cared, figuring one day they might marry.

Cassie and her fiancé would be seeing Si in a *A Tale of Two Cities,* the Play House's adaptation of Charles Dickens' novel set in London and Paris during the French Revolution.

The play depicts a love triangle: two men, Charles Darnay and Sydney Carton, in love with the same woman, Lucie Manette.

Si, who found himself in a love triangle, decided to give his best performance ever as Sydney Carton, the drunken, aimless lawyer.

He would make Cassie think, *My God, his performance is about me.* He would let her know how much she inspired him.

Si readied himself. That night, he felt his makeup was beautiful and his costume perfect. He stood on his mark and delivered his first line.

"Look to that young lady, she's fainted," he said.

The line fell flat.

The play carried on. Darnay married Lucie and returned to Paris. The nephew of a despised marquis, Darnay was unjustly thrown in prison and sentenced to the guillotine.

Since he resembled Darnay, Carton decided to take his place in prison and give his life so Lucie would be happy, an ultimate act of love. Carton slipped into prison, drugged Darnay and had him spirited away.

A Tale of Two Cities builds to the beheading of Carton. On good nights, the Play House audience tenses with the anticipation of the climax and the delivery by Carton of some of the most famous lines in the English language.

That night, Si felt he hadn't mustered even a passable performance. At the climax, the audience seemed dead. Si heard the vexing tinkle of impatient people fingering their car keys.

Then he declaimed those famous, closing words:

"It is a far, far better thing that I do, than I have ever done. It is a far, far better rest that I go to than I have ever known."

Curtain, curtain call and polite applause.

Afterward, Si met Cassie and her fiancé for a drink at the Boarding House. The fiancé was a nice, steady guy, a banker.

"What was the problem with the guy you were playing?" Cassie asked Si. "Was he in love or something? You looked anguished all the way through."

Jeez, my acting was so bad that she missed part of the plot, Si thought.

"Yeah, Cassie," Si replied. "He was in love with a girl he couldn't get."

When they left the nightclub and walked to their cars, Cassie called out: "We'll come to your next play. What is it?"

"A light British comedy," he said.

"Oh, *that* should be fun," she said, unintentionally.

Si returned to his tiny apartment and pulled down the Murphy bed. Sleep would not come. He got up and went to the window

nd looked out over Lake View Cemetery, fixing his gaze on a
ray stone angel.

He knew he had lost something this night. He stared at the an-
;el's upturned hand as it gathered the lightly falling snow and a
ine from *A Tale of Two Cities* played over and over in his head:

"No man ever really loved a woman, lost her, and then stopped
oving her when she became a wife and mother."

February 25, 1983

Changing himself

Lovell doesn't hang with the gang anymore.

He doesn't loiter in front of W & W Foods on E. 105th Street. He doesn't get into silly fights or weave his bike in traffic or get stoned.

"Hey, Lovell, let's smoke some reefer," they still tell him.

"Let's ride around and pick up some freaks," they suggest.

"Wanna get high, man?" they inquire.

Lovell Reddick, fifteen years old, just smiles and shrugs, "No thanks."

"I'm not in the mood for no trouble," he explained yesterday. "I just stay here or play basketball at the rec center."

Lovell and his sister, Vita, nineteen, were sitting at a big table in a house tucked into the back of a storefront on E. 105th. Lovell was wearing a clean white polo shirt, pressed blue jeans and boating shoes without socks. He looked preppy. Vita wore a red T-shirt, jeans and house slippers.

"He's changed a whole lot now," she said. "Now we see him through the day. The boys he hung around with on the corner, they're not his type."

Last summer, Lovell would get up in the morning, eat a bowl of cereal or toast, then walk to the corner and buy a newspaper for his mother. He'd bring it back, get on his bicycle and disappear until eleven at night.

This worried his mother, Willie Mae Reddick. He was her youngest, and he seemed headed down a wrong path. She had had it rough raising her five kids since her husband left years ago.

There were better places to raise her son than this stretch of E. 105th in Glenville. By mid-afternoon, men gather across the street from where Lovell used to hang out. She didn't like the example these men set for the world to see. They would drink and smoke marijuana and cadge quarters from the kids for more quarts of beer.

Two weeks ago, the day after Lovell came home from six weeks at the military academy, he surprised everybody. He looked at the narrow empty lot next to the house. It was filled with weeds and bottles and wrappers. Without a word, he went to work, plucking the weeds and picking up the trash.

Recalling this story yesterday, Willie Mae Reddick seemed ready to cry. She had just returned from church and found Lovell and Vita at the table talking to a reporter.

"It was really the most touching thing," she said. "He really grew up. It just made my chest stick out real far."

She sent Lovell back to his room to fetch the certificates and awards and letter that explained his changes.

One certificate was headed with the words "Vocational Information Program." Lovell had enrolled in the respected career counseling program for inner-city kids in junior high school. He was tutored in math on Saturdays by Max Slavin, a retired real estate man.

Lovell's grades picked up. He applied for a program scholarship to the prestigious Culver Military Academy in Indiana. To his surprise, he won.

Lovell had never seen anything like Culver. He was one of eight blacks out of 1,300 students. The summer students, aged fifteen to seventeen, came from all over the world: Spain, Germany, Venezuela, Puerto Rico. One boy said he was the nephew of a king.

Lovell took lessons in algebra, English, sailing and swimming. The swimming posed a little problem at first.

He didn't want to get his longish hair cut. So he slicked it back with grease. The first time in the pool, his hair frizzed out and left an oil slick on the water. He had to get a haircut the next day.

Because of the Vocational Information Program, Lovell has decided he'd like to learn about aviation, join the Air Force and be a pilot someday.

Meanwhile, he's got his school supplies ready for tenth grade, which he starts September 7 at West Tech High School.

"High-class man," the old gang calls Lovell.
"You're in the books now," they jibe him.
"You act like you don't know us," they say.

Wouldn't it be a lot easier to get high and hang on the corner? Lovell was asked.

He smiled and sheepishly nodded yes.

"But I don't want to be like them," he said. "I want to be somebody. I got too much going for me now."

August 15, 1983

The kindest cut

Snip snip snip.

Harry Byers, probably the city's oldest active barber, was at work. His fingers flashed comb and scissors near Billy Evans' aged right ear.

Snip snip snip.

His hands hovered like huge hummingbirds around the customer's head. Clarence, the old jeweler across the hall, came in and saw Evans perched on the ancient porcelain-handled barber chair.

"What you doing getting your hair cut, Billy?" Clarence said. "You got nothing to cut."

Evans was lucky. He was getting one of the last haircuts in Byers' sixty-year career. Harry B. Byers — the carriage trade barber whose sharp scissors have cut the hair of bankers and bookies, politicians and policemen — is throwing in the hot towel.

"I'm not retiring because I don't have the business," said Byers, who will soon turn eighty. "I'm stopping because I don't have many more years left. It's a hard thing to say I'm gonna stop.

"My wife's pet slogan is, 'Quit while the band's still playing.' Guess you know what she means by that."

Tomorrow, from 11 a.m. to 4 p.m., "Harry's fellahs" will be stopping by the tiny third-floor barbershop at 1110 Euclid Avenue for an open house. Some of the guys, Phil Lustig, Fred Ball, E. J. Weardon, are the third generation in their families to be groomed by Byers.

He is a remarkable-looking old guy. He moves gracefully around the barber chair. A few lines furrow his brow and crinkle the skin around his eyes. He looks like a man of sixty who has lost most of his hair and wears a brushy silver mustache to balance his features.

His formal yet warm manners are a throwback to a simpler time when etiquette mattered. He is the last of an era, an old-time southern gentlemen, an elegant black man who wanted to become a doctor. He came from a poor Alabama family, and made it as far as his junior year at Selma University before giving up his dream of wielding a surgeon's knife and settling instead on the straight razor.

He was working for two doctors, cleaning their offices and running errands. He had asked them to help put him through school. But they were selfish; they refused him.

"It still gets me provoked when I think about it," Byers said plainly, a rare show of pique for this most even-tempered of men.

For seven years he worked as a barber on a Great Lakes ship. For seventeen years he worked in an Ashtabula barber shop. On May 6, 1946, he bought the shop he will retire from at month's end.

Byers never advertised. It would have been a waste of money. Guys used to have to wait two or three days to get an appointment.

"Gramps' barbershop was a place to go for therapy," said Christine Branch, a school administrator who is his stepdaughter. "He was privy to the thoughts and plans and thinking processes of those who made this city. The relationships then developed in a very different way. It was a small shop. There were one-to-one relationships. It's not like today, where barbers want to get you in and out."

Then the Gillette safety razor blade changed the pace and measure of the barbering business. Men wanted only haircuts, and those post-World War II styles took only minutes. The barbershop as a gentlemen's club slowly died out.

"You in a hurry?" Byers asked a visitor a day or two ago. "Get up in this chair and I'll show you what we old-time barbers are all about."

He took off the guy's glasses and wrapped the man's face in a hot towel. When the coarse white towel cooled off, Byers replaced it with another and then another.

The old barber picked up a stainless steel straight razor and flicked it back and forth across a leather strop, bringing out a fine edge.

"Shaving is quite an art," Byers said. "If you can shave a man without hurting him, it's a great feeling."

The visitor was lying back in the old chair. Byers took the towel off and started sliding the razor across the whiskers, starting at the sideburns and working down to the neck, occasionally turning the man's head with sure, swift hands.

"If you couldn't shave a man you weren't much of a barber," Byers went on.

That was the old days when a barber and his customer had a special relationship. You had to trust the man who pulled a razor back and forth across your throat.

Byers finished the blade work and splashed on lotion and administered a facial massage. He rubbed on witch hazel.

"How's that feel?" he asked.

"Great," came the reply.

Byers was finished for the day. He would go to his co-op apartment on East Boulevard, where he lives with his wife, Kitty, who used to run a high-class catering business. Now they are both retired and looking forward to fishing at their cottage in Canada and spending time with their children and grandchildren.

Tap tap tap.

"I've been a lucky guy," Byers said, rapping his knuckles on a window sill in his shop. "I've had a wonderful trade."

July 22, 1982

A triumph of love

Judge Howard Douglas returned to his chamber and picked up a telephone message: *Alice Darling called.*

That name hit him like a punch. He hadn't heard from Alice Darling in nearly fifty years. Why, he used to wait outside her parent's house in the cold mornings of Brattleboro, Vermont. When she came out, he would heft her school bag and walk her to high school along the narrow country roads.

Howard and Alice were sweethearts. He was tall, 6-feet-6, thin as a willow branch and nicknamed Slim. She was petite and wore long, dark braids wrapped demurely around her head. Slim was straight as an arrow; she was adventurous.

Alice's father worked for the telephone company and got her a summer job. She worked her way through college tacking numbered metal plates to phone poles. Accompanied by her German shepherd, she sometimes walked more than twenty miles a day, earning fifteen cents for each pole she branded.

Vermont was dry then, and once in a while, as a favor, Alice delivered Canadian whiskey smuggled into Brattleboro to a man upstate who supplied a country club. The politicians and bankers spurned the hard apple cider favored by the country folk.

When the police told her father she had to quit driving around with whiskey in the car, Alice decided she needed a change. She packed her bags, took a train to Cleveland and enrolled at Western Reserve University. After she earned her degree, she worked in the loan department at Cleveland Trust Company.

Slim was teaching civics in high school in Rutland, Vermont. He tried to keep their romance going. But Alice was determined to pull up her country roots forever and carve out a career in the big city.

Slim sent her a letter. It said: "Come and claim your property or I'm going to marry the school librarian."

Alice wasn't ready to claim him as her property. She was twenty-three and didn't want to move back to Vermont. She wrote back: "Pleasant journeys and happy landings."

Slim married the school librarian. He continued to teach. He ran for alderman and won. He was stern and independent, forever questioning policies and projects, a Yankee version of Socrates. After thirteen years as alderman, he ran for probate judge. To his surprise, he won.

Meanwhile, Alice worked at Cleveland Trust until her supervisor was promoted. She asked for his job.

"A woman will never hold that job," the head of personnel told her.

She left, went to work at Halle's, then at the office of the Catholic Diocese. At thirty-one, she married Joseph Strobel, a tool and die maker.

A few years ago, Alice took a vacation to the coast of Spain. Her husband had died in 1974. Her three children were grown and she lived alone.

"I'm from Vermont, too," Alice told a woman on the tour. "Do you know Slim Douglas?"

"Do you mean Judge Howard Douglas?" the woman replied. "I worked with him."

Alice and the woman became friends. When Alice returned to visit her in Vermont, she called Slim.

The judge had never gotten over her. When he finally talked to her, he didn't know what to say.

"This is the first time I've ever talked to you on a telephone," he managed.

He asked Alice to go with him to visit his wife in the hospital. She died last year on Alice's birthday, June 14.

At the Green Mountain College campus, a week after his wife's death, they were sitting on a bench by a fountain. "Will you marry me?" the judge asked softly.

"What? Of course not," she replied.

Three months ago, Slim and Alice, both seventy-three, got married and went on a honeymoon to Maine.

Yesterday, in their old stone house on Green Road, they reminisced about their reunion.

"I invited you up to the hospital because I didn't want Barbara to think I was going behind her back," he said.

Alice looked at him fondly. "She trusted you. She never had a thought like that, Slim."

She turned to a vistor. "Barbara was such a beautiful person. Actually, Slim, you had a beautiful life, which you probably wouldn't have had with a scrapper like me."

"You gave me a hard time at your graduation," he recalled. "You said you were going to marry somebody else."

"Did I already have your pin?"

"You were a very hard person to get to," he went on.

"I didn't think you were really wildly amorous," Alice said. "We would hold hands and kiss as far as I remember."

"Yes."

"Don't you like excitement?" she teased.

"No," Slim answered with a wry smile. "That's why I married you."

January 13, 1983

The justice buff

Tony the Trial Watcher takes a seat in Judge David Matia's courtroom and waits for the verdict.

"What do you think, Tony?" someone asks the old man. Will Leonard Jenkins, the guy convicted of murdering a policeman during a bank robbery, get the electric chair?

Tony replies without hesitation, "Life and thirty years, no parole."

In the hustle-bustle world of the Justice Center, Tony is a constant. He has not missed a week of watching trials since he retired from the railroad in 1972.

In these carpeted courtrooms, reputations are made and destroyed. People are set free and locked up. Marriages are sundered. Families are reunited. People weep or rejoice at the turns in their fortunes.

Taking it all in, quietly sitting as if in a pew in a cathedral, is Tony the Trial Watcher.

He pads down the Justice Center hallways with a slow, stiff-kneed shuffle, his short, stout bulk draped in a rumpled black overcoat. In his hand, he holds a black hat that he pops on his hairless head once he gets outside.

What they don't know is that Tony's last name is Dinardo and that he is seventy-seven and lives at 2265 E. 127th Street with his wife and a daughter and a granddaughter.

Tony came here in 1922 from a southern Italian village near Naples. He is one U.S. citizen who understands better than most lawyers how the justice system works in our town.

Tony said he learned to speak his adopted tongue by attending trials. But there is no mistaking his English for Clarence Darrow's. Tony's tongue rolls stubbornly over the words, dropping final syllables like a clumsy bricklayer.

"I come to trials to enjoy myself," said Tony. "I like to hear lawyers talk. I like to hear how prosecutors talk. I been come around since 1937."

Tony was laid off of his sewer-digging job that year. So he decided to see what was happening to five men accused of killing two Cleveland cops. It was a sensational trial in which two defendants were sentenced to the electric chair. One of the five was 16-year-old Anthony Liberatore, now on trial for the bombing murder of racketeer Danny Greene. Liberatore was sentenced to the chair back in that old trial, but was granted mercy since he was young and had a wife and family.

The Justice Center regulars know Tony by his first name. Judges and lawyers ask his opinion. On slow days, reporters rely on him to tell them what's going on.

He talks to whoever will listen. After Chico Morales was found guilty of murdering Tammy Seals, Tony walked down a hallway, never slowing down, saying: "Thatta verdict stink! Thatta verdict stink!"

Tony's routine is as unvarying as the change of seasons. At his home, he arises weekdays, eats breakfast, puts on a coat and a tie and catches the bus on the corner. He reads the morning paper and usually knows which courtroom he'll go to when he arrives at the Justice Center around 9:30. He favors the drama of murder and rape trials.

At noon, when courts usually recess, Tony goes to the Society for the Blind's coffee shop on the fourth floor. He buys a 25-cent cup of coffee and takes a table with a couple of other old-time trial watchers. They talk trials, swap stories, always looking out for a juicier case to occupy them that afternoon. But the ranks of the dedicated trial watchers are thinning.

"A couple favorite guys died," Tony lamented. "Harry Watson died. Another guy, Jackson, died. One died January 25. The other died 1979."

Tony has seen the big ones — one Sheppard trial, the Judge Steele murder case, the first Danny Greene case. Usually he avoids the federal courtrooms. He doesn't like being searched on the way in. "I no like that," he said. "I hate that."

While others his age may be content to stay home and watch soap operas, Tony insists on getting out.

"I don't like to stay home," he said. "I get sick if I stay home."

He has his favorite judges: Leo Spellacy, the Matias, Francis

Sweeney. "I talk to them," he said. "I am much friendly with these judges."

His favorite lawyers? "I likka Jerry Milano," Tony said. "He's a good criminal lawyer. I likka Ralph Sperli. He's a good criminal lawyer. I likka Elmer Giuliani. He's a good criminal lawyer."

Tony looks at his watch and sees that it is time to catch his 3:50 bus. He has waited all day and will miss the Jenkins verdict.

He shuffles out of the courtoom and walks to the elevators. He sees Jenkins' mother, goes over and shakes her hand.

"I wish you luck, lady," he said. "I wish you luck."

April 12, 1982

Driven by despair

He probably wasn't certain when he would fire the handgun that day. He had snitched the key and unlocked a cabinet in his father's bedroom the night before and had removed the .25-caliber pistol.

He could conceal it in his palm. He was seventeen but had never fired a gun before, and it took him a while to figure out how to insert the ammunition magazine.

The boy — call him Tommy — usually rode a yellow school bus to Lorain High School, where he was a junior. But last Thursday he told his mom he wanted to walk.

He walked west on Colorado Avenue, then along the railroad tracks that cross the Black River and pass four blocks from school. Tommy was carrying his Bible, a birthday card, a love letter, his school lunch pass — and the gun.

At first, he thought he would shoot the gun in the library. But for reasons still unclear, he didn't. At 10:30 a.m., the beginning of the first lunch period, he walked into the cafeteria and went to a table where he knew some people.

Tommy handed his Bible to a boy at the next table. Tommy also handed him the cross he wore and a love letter. He asked the boy to mail it to a girl in Avon Lake whom he knew from his Bible classes at the Baptist church. He gave the birthday card to a teacher and asked him to give it to a girl who rode the bus with him.

Tommy didn't know the girl on the bus very well. He didn't know anyone at Lorain High very well. His family moved to Lorain from New London last summer. This was the third school he had attended in as many years.

Tommy sat down in one of the orange and yellow plastic chairs at a long table. About a half-dozen students were there.

"I won't be needing this," he said, and handed his lunch ticket to a friend.

Concealing the gun in his hand under the table, Tommy waited a few minutes. Then he pointed it and fired.

The three hundred or so students in the lunch room heard a muffled *pop* as the bullet tore into Tommy's stomach two inches above his navel.

Kids started screaming and some ran to the principal's office yelling, "Somebody's been shot."

"Seal the doors," an assistant principal announced over the public address system. "Please be calm."

Tommy was sped to St. Joseph Hospital, where surgeons worked furiously to save the life Tommy had tried to snuff out. He remains in critical condition.

Capt. Michael Kocak, a kind, softspoken detective with white hair, was assigned to look into the incident. Kocak was puzzled. The boy came from a devout family. He had good grades. He had never been in trouble at school.

The detective went to the hospital. "Why did you do it?" he asked Tommy.

"The days are awful long," the boy said. "I don't have anybody to talk to."

Tommy did try to talk to people. He was a devout Baptist and would go on about the Bible and its message to whoever would listen. He was not handsome or fashionably dressed or able to talk about rock bands or current movies. He was the only boy in a "Family Living" class with dozens of girls. Some of the guys thought this was weird.

Some of his classmates thought he was "a nerd" or was "out of it." To his face or behind his back, some derisively called him "preacher man."

Tommy's dad said this hurt his son.

"He tried to get them to witness and they put him down," Tommy's father said yesterday. "They told him to go away, they didn't want him at their table."

Tommy's father is a short, stout man with an Abe Lincoln beard. He wears green work pants and work shirts that are popular at the Lorain Ford plant, where he has worked for the twenty-two years since he brought his family to Ohio from West Virginia.

"Some of these girls stay out all hours of the night and they think they're so good and they put him down," he went on. "I don't care to repeat some of the things they said."

Did this have anything to do with the shooting? Tommy's dad was asked.

"I think so," the man replied. "I haven't talked to the boy about it yet."

"Kids can be cruel these days," Kocak, the detective, said later. "Kids will make fun of somebody who's cross-eyed, crippled, with some physical ailment. They can really hit home."

When Tommy goes back to Lorain High School, you can bet the kids won't feel like teasing him anymore. Tommy will be different, too.

"I pushed the Bible too hard," he told the detective. "I won't do it anymore when I get back to school."

March 25, 1982

Sin's alternative

Sonny Jones never gave the Baptist church across the street much thought. At closing time, when he locked his nightclub, the church sat dark and still, a sharp contrast to the frenzy of con men and street pushers working Kinsman Road at all hours.

Sonny's club, the Kinsman Grill, 12803 Kinsman Road, was a magnet for night people. Nearby, the Shrimp Boat and Mt. Pleasant Barbecue drew traffic to the area, too, providing customers and cover for the hustlers.

The club made sweet paydays for Sonny in the 1970s. Kinsman Dazz, now a Grammy award winner, served as house band. Sonny was manager of the group when it grabbed a major recording contract.

Around 1979, like maggots crawling to decaying meat, dope sellers made the two blocks on either side of his nightclub into a free-wheeling drugstore.

"It was like a supermarket," Sonny said. "There were thirty people selling drugs on the corner. Our older customers started to desert us. The drug people were crossing each other. There were a lot of shootings. It was crazy.

"Gradually, they infiltrated my place. The community was blaming my place as the nucleus of the problem."

To the church folks and residents of the Mt. Pleasant neighborhood, Sonny Jones, forty-five, looked like a big-time pimp or dope dealer. He drove a 1954 Bentley. His wrists and fingers dazzled with $8,000 worth of gold and diamond jewelry. Around his neck, he wore a silver scorpion, its tail shaped into a coke spoon.

"The way I was living, man, it was sinful," he said. "I didn't think nothing of having four, five women."

He didn't mess much with drink or drugs. "I always thought I was a good guy," he said. "I wouldn't kill nobody or steal nothing."

For five years, he worked as a city fire fighter. He pulled two kids out of a burning ghetto home on May 6, 1976, and was awarded the Medal of Valor.

He was living a double life and it nearly killed him. One night, at the bar, a woman pulled out a gun, waved it and said she would shoot the waitress.

Sonny knew the young woman. Her husband had died recently. She was drunk.

As his patrons scattered, Sonny said, "If you want to shoot somebody, shoot me."

She put the gun to his head, cussed him out, and capped off two shots into the ceiling.

Working on a pumper truck the next day, Sonny was dispatched to the Garden Valley housing projects. A fire was crackling moderately in an apartment, held in check by lack of oxygen; the windows hadn't been punched in yet.

Sonny crawled inside, searching for victims. He heard the windows being axed. He knew what would happen next. Fed by fresh air, the apartment burst into a fireball. Only a quick, heavy stream from a pumper saved him.

Sonny had a realization: "I'm messing with the law of averages. One thing is gonna have to go."

He hung up the hoses and hip-boots.

Last year, he began to have doubts about the nightclub.

"People would come in with their last few dollars," he explained. "They were frustrated, used to working at Ford, Chevrolet, making good money. All it would take was someone to say Boo! and we had a big fight. You sit up here and feed people alcohol. You know they're going to turn into monsters. But you keep feeding them because it's your job."

When an old friend died, Sonny went for the first time to Providence Baptist Church across the street for the funeral. He heard the Rev. Rodney Maiden preach. Sonny got to know the 30-year-old pastor better at neighborhood safety meetings begun last year to curb crime in Mt. Pleasant.

The low-key pastor, who had clocked some street time himself, impressed Sonny. He started going to services.

In April, Sonny was baptized and the 580-member congregation rejoiced. But months later, a guy on the street accosted Sonny: "Man, we know you go to church. Then you come over here and sell alcohol. You're a hypocrite."

It made sense. Sonny decided to close one of the city's famous night spots last November.

Business boomed in October. The last week of the month, usually slow, was one of Sonny's best.

"I think that Satan had something to do with that," he said. "He didn't want to lose me."

Sonny shuttered his meal ticket anyway.

Next month, Sonny Jones will reopen his club as The Alternative. It will feature top gospel acts and serve soft drinks and fruit juices.

"Since Sonny shut the old place down, it's been a great help," said the pastor. "The drugs maybe have gone underground. Most of the guys out there know Sonny. His change has been great for the neighborhood."

January 12, 1984

Repaying a debt

Across the tiny, old cemetery on Wilson Mills Road she walked, a flat of marigolds and a shiny trowel in hand.

All around her, poking through the thick grass like well-worn teeth, were sun-bleached sandstone markers no bigger than a Bible. Gray marble obelisks cast shadows of different sizes on miniature American flags that fluttered in the late May breeze.

Long before she reached the unmarked graves of her husband's parents, she saw the bright red flowers.

Under the drooping pine boughs sat a small stone urn, the only thing marking the Swaffield graves. It was overflowing with blooming red geraniums. The usual tangle of pine needles and cones had been swept up.

"What is this?" Maree Swaffield wondered. "Who is taking care of our plots?"

She pondered the mystery of the flowers as she drove to her Wickliffe home. She called her husband's only two cousins in Cleveland to thank them for the flowers. But they did not plant them.

"I live so far away," said the one who lives in Old Brooklyn. "I haven't been coming over on that side."

Maree Swaffield, now sixty-two, was puzzled. She began visiting the gravesite at the Mayfield Union Cemetery more often. Each time the pine needles were picked up and the dead leaves carefully pinched off the red flowers. Who could be doing this?

In the early fall of that year, on the afternoon of the first forecasted frost, Maree drove to the cemetery. She was going to dig up the red geraniums before the frost killed them.

She found her urn empty, its soil freshly overturned and leveled only hours earlier.

The next Memorial Day, Maree visited the cemetery. She saw a woman with garden tools planting geraniums in the unmarked Swaffield urn. The woman was tall and thin and sturdy looking, with gray hair and a face etched with sadness.

"You're the one taking care of our plots," Swaffield told her. "I want to thank you. My husband's family is buried here."

The woman apologized. She said her name was Ludmilla Fisher and apologized again. She pointed to two Fisher gravestones next to the plot with the urn. Ludmilla said she had thought the urn marked her husband's parents' plots and so she had been planting the flowers.

The two women began to talk. Ludmilla explained how she and her husband had done everything together and how she had been lonely these seven years since his death.

"Would you like to see his grave?" she asked Maree. They walked about twenty yards to four squat marble headstones. Three were inscribed with the names of her husband and his parents. The fourth headstone was blank.

Ludmilla had planted red geraniums here, too. She said she and her husband loved the geraniums because the bright red could be spotted from the street. "It's our wish that our family always keep the geraniums here," Ludmilla told Maree.

A year later when Maree Swaffield visited the cemetery, she noticed that the red geraniums were missing from the Fisher headstones near the urn. Maree had a strange feeling.

She walked over to the four headstones Ludmilla had shown her before. There were no flowers. Heavy grass and leaves cluttered the plot.

The fourth headstone was no longer blank. It read: Ludmilla Fisher 1909-1978.

Each year after that, Maree Swaffield checked the plots of Ludmilla Fisher and her relatives. "This will be the year that her family will have planted the red geraniums," Maree thought each year.

But flowers were never planted. At last she realized that the surviving Fishers did not know of Ludmilla's wishes or else didn't care.

This weekend, Maree Swaffield bought some bright red geraniums. She carried them in a peck basket with a watering can and a trowel to the Fisher gravesites.

She turned the moist soil with a trowel and made a hole for the flowers. She removed them from the green plastic pots and planted them, pressing the soil all around.

Maree stood up and gazed down at red blossoms that were beginning to open.

"Ludmilla, we owed you one," she said.

May 30, 1983

A polished career

Each workday morning, Van C. Dillard catches the 28X bus in Euclid and gets off at Public Square shortly before noon. He walks over to a small storefront connected to the Ontario Lounge.

Inside, a small deli counter sells takeout sandwiches. A steady stream of people buy lottery tickets from a young guy named Mark. Occupying a corner is Dillard's worn meal ticket: a shoeshine stand — basically, a chair on a stepped platform with two shiny steel footrests.

Dillard puts his gym bag full of supplies under the stand, arranges his old black suit coat on the back of the elevated chair and sets his straw hat on an old kitchen table. He's ready for work.

"This is just to keep active," he explained. "I'm seventy-three. It's been a good life. I met so many fine people. I raised two kids. They got good educations and got good jobs."

Dillard is a broad, slightly stoop-shouldered man with a remarkably unlined face and a full head of hair. He bent over slowly and pulled from the bag an autograph book with a page for each day of the year. He slowly flipped through the pages; the faded fountain pen scrawls sent him on a nostalgic trip.

"What's that say?" he asked, pointing to the page marked September 28.

It reads: "Best wishes to you and here's to a pennant in 1953. Jimmy Dudley."

The pages contain the names of the wheels, the wealthy and the well-known who passed through Dillard's shoe shine parlor in the Hotel Cleveland (now Stouffer's Inn on the Square), where he worked from 1927 to 1960. He's polished the shoes of Philadelphia Athletics owner Connie Mack, industrialist Cyrus Eaton, editor Louis Seltzer, Indians owner Alva Bradley, Babe Ruth, Casey

Stengel and dozens of other baseball and football players, Bobo
Newsom, Allie "Superchief" Reynolds, Eddie "the Walking Man"
Yost, Bobby Avila, Thurman McGraw, Joe Stydahar.
Dillard seems to have a story about each.
"Babe Ruth, he was up on the ninth floor, him and his buddy,"
Dillard said. "It was the opening of the Stadium. Babe Ruth said,
'That's no ballpark. That's a damn cow pasture.' You see, this was
before they put the fences up at the Stadium."
When President Eisenhower stayed at the Hotel Cleveland, Dil-
lard polished his shoes. Nikita Khrushchev's, too.
"I saw a woman throw a tomato at Khrushchev," Dillard re-
membered, chuckling. "Some people were tickled to death."
For several years, Dillard sent a birthday card to everyone in his
book. This was a good business practice until postage became too
expensive. Early Wynn, the ball player, got a card in Florida one
year. Wynn went around asking, "Who's Van in the Hotel
Cleveland?"
"He shines your shoes," Wynn was told.
Dillard was successful. At one time he had two men working at
his shoeshine concession. He set up what he called a cosmetic bar,
selling combs and razor blades, cologne and toothbrushes. His
clients were the guys on dates at the big band dances in the hotel's
Bronze Room.
"Excuse me," he told his visitor, moving toward the shop's door.
A car had pulled up outside. "Hey, let's get busy," Dillard kidded
Mark, the agent behind the lottery machine. They went to the
trunk of the car blocking traffic and brought in a couple of cases
of booze for the lounge.
"My best year was 1948," he resumed. "The Indians were in the
World Series. That was my year. I kept the shop open twenty-four
hours a day. A lot of people don't know what it's like to have the
World Series in this town. '54 was good. But see, they lost four
straight. Willie Mays killed us. Boy, he robbed us."
Dillard put the book aside and told his visitor he wanted to sell
it. He wants to move out of his grandson's house in Euclid and in-
to the Bohn Tower downtown, the subsidized high-rise for elderly.
Dillard said he could use the extra cash from selling the book.
"I have about five customers a day," he said. "Sometimes two or
three."
He charges a dollar, ten times the going rate when he started in
1927, four times his 1960 price.
"Used to be, a man wouldn't go out on the street without his

shoes shined," he said. "I think that's coming back."

A heavyset woman walked in and took her place in the lottery ticket line. "How you feel?" she asked Dillard.

"Fine, honey," he replied.

"No luck yet," she told him.

"Don't worry," he said. "Keep on playing."

August 25, 1983

A new start

He slouched in the back of the limousine, his fingers laced across his belly and his legs out straight.

"Like my caddy?" he asked. "It's a good toy."

Roger Martin was zipping along the Ohio Turnpike to Ponderosa Park in Salem, Ohio, where he was the opening act yesterday for Nashville country star Ronnie McDowell.

Martin was like a kid on Christmas Day with his new trappings of success: a mint condition 1966 Fleetwood Cadillac limo with a built-in color TV, a pair of $300 Justin cowboy boots on his feet, a driver and, in the new Toronado following behind, a manager with money to invest.

But where's your stash? The coke and smack, the syringes and cooker spoons, the scabbed arms and hyped eyes?

"I'm clean, man," Martin insisted, holding out his arms for inspection. "You won't find a pin cushion on me. No, baby. That's out. Out!"

So this is the new Roger Martin?

"I haven't touched a syringe in five months," he said. "You know how I miss it? I dream about it at night. It's like an old love."

Roger Vitorrio Martin, thirty-two, is easily the Cleveland area's best country singer and entertainer. He's a decorated and disabled Vietnam veteran, a black belt and the self-described "Italian Cowboy," son of a Sicilian immigrant and a West Virginia coal miner.

Add to the list: reformed junkie and member of Alcoholics Anonymous.

Sure, we've heard it all before. Roger Martin has put the touch on nearly every friend, honky-tonk owner and booker in town: "I'm clean, man. I've got it together. C'mon, loan me a hundred.

Give me a break."

He's been in and out of hospitals, cooling out on Methadone or drying out cold turkey, eight or nine times in as many years. This time, he says it's for good. Old friends, who've been burned by him before, believe him.

"He's been straight," said Big Darlene, an old flame. "He sounds as good as he did six, seven years ago."

Last August, Roger Martin hit bottom. He was badly strung out, injecting prescriptive opiates like Dilaudid and Talwin, drinking heavily and losing his mind.

"I was going to jail five times a week, fighting, breaking the windows out of my house, acting like a little brat," he said.

Kenny Moore, a friend of Martin's sister in Alcoholics Anonymous, came over to the Eastlake home where Martin lives with his wife, Pat, and son, Roger Jr.

Moore talked to him about A.A. "He got me at the right time," Martin said.

"I checked into an alcoholism clinic in Youngstown for thirty days. I came out feeling like a million bucks. Then I slipped. I had one drink. One drink ticked me off.

"Being an alcoholic and working in bars is rough," he said. "It's like being hungry in a grocery store."

He fought back. He changed his phone number so the cocaine man couldn't call.

"I sent his kids through college," Martin said. "I sent his mother to Europe. He wasn't getting anything more from me."

Since then, he hasn't missed a gig.

At the outdoor pavilion at Ponderosa Park, Martin and his band took the stage about 1:30 p.m. and sparked the family crowd. People clapped along to his "Orange Blossom Special" and cheered his medley of Hank Williams Sr. songs.

Martin's 12-year-old son wandered through the aisles, displaying over his head black-and-white glossies of his dad and selling them for a dollar each.

An older woman with a cane and gray curls called the boy over, bought a photo, and slipped it into her program. It was the first of more than one hundred sold.

Last summer, stoned out of his mind, Martin insulted a Ponderosa Park crowd with obscenities and a dreadful performance. Yesterday, he seemed to win them back.

He ran though a medley of near-perfect imitations of country music greats like Hank Snow, Ernest Tubb and Marty Robbins.

Then a middle-aged man in the crowd walked to the stage and told Martin over the microphone: "Glad to see you back from the shape you were in."

The crowd applauded and Martin yelled, "Yeeiiii!"

"I'm not the man I could be," he said, thanking the crowd at the end. "I'm not the man I should be. Thank God I'm not the man I used to be."

June 6, 1983

Past revisited

John Sopko was in bed asleep in his rundown apartment on Murray Hill when shock waves from the blast knocked him to the floor.

The next morning, on his way to law school classes at Case Western Reserve University, he learned what had happened. Some garbage trucks belonging to Mike Frato had been bombed. Authorities had a suspect: Danny Greene, the flamboyant racketeer who was trying to muscle control of the rubbish hauling business.

Sopko didn't know at the time that Greene and Teamster official John Nardi were trying to take over the Cleveland mob from its interim head, James Licavoli, known as Jack White.

On his way to school, Sopko occasionally would pass a short, stooped man with a cane sitting outside the Card Shop or the Italian American Brotherhood Club on Mayfield Road. He didn't know that this little man was Licavoli, the *capo* of the Cleveland regime, and that the top of the cane unscrewed to reveal an 18-inch stiletto.

It was 1975, and Sopko was just another law student trying to make good grades and land a job. He had no idea that seven years later, in July 1982, he would know all about Jack White and Danny Greene and John Nardi.

He had no idea that he would be the 30-year-old Strike Force prosecutor who helped finally convict 77-year-old Licavoli — virtually untouchable since bootlegging days — and five of his soldiers for their roles in the bombing murder of Greene.

"That's got to be Licavoli's son," Sopko's mother-in-law told him when she heard about the trial. She grew up in Detroit and remembered the name Licavoli from newspaper accounts of the Purple Gang, infamous bootleggers and extortionists.

It was James Licavoli, the one and only, offspring of the notorious Licavoli family in St. Louis that still controls rackets in St. Louis, Toledo and Detroit.

By the time he left St. Louis for Detroit in 1926, Licavoli had been arrested at least fifteen times and wounded during a police chase. Between 1926 and 1938, this young man was arrested two dozen times for everything from bootlegging to weapons charges. Through the crime family's influence and wealth, he served only a year or two in prison.

Throughout this last trial, Sopko thought the canny old man probably would get off again.

Sopko's co-counsel during the trial, the venerable Abe Poretz, seventy, prepared the closing arguments. Poretz had been through this hundreds of times and is a master. He planned to carry on eloquently about justice and society and the public good.

Sopko suggested he describe defendants Licavoli, Anthony Liberatore and the others as generals in an army.

"You've got the privates and the generals," Sopko recounted later. "Although the privates are on the lines, somebody's back in headquarters directing it. So it's not just the hit men out there committing the crimes. About seven of the guys on the jury were of World War II and Korean War age and I thought they'd relate to the analogy."

Poretz used his advice. It didn't hurt. All six defendants were found guilty.

This was Sopko's last hurrah here. The day after tomorrow, he is leaving Cleveland and the Strike Force behind. He and his wife, Joan, are moving to Washington, where he will be a minority counsel for the Senate Permanent Subcommittee on Investigations, a great job for a 30-year-old lawyer.

He knows he is walking away from the Strike Force when his career there is at a peak. "Crime's always going to be with us," he said. "I just want something different."

Two days ago, he bought his secretary a farewell lunch at a University Circle restaurant. Still buoyant after the six guilty verdicts last week, he was taking off the rest of the afternoon and she was dropping him off at his Cleveland Heights home.

They were driving up Mayfield Road through Little Italy when Sopko said, "Hey, there's Jack!"

Sitting in front of the Card Shop, the reputed gambling and loan shark operation, was Licavoli. Out on appeals bond, Licavoli and another old *paisan* were watching traffic go by. Between his legs, the don was holding his cherished cane.

They slowed down, and Sopko waved to the Mafioso he had helped put away.

Licavoli looked up and recognized the young man who had sat across from him in the courtroom for twelve weeks. The old man smiled, lifted his hand and waved back.

July 15, 1982

Never forget

Her waking memories are the stuff of nightmares:

A man amputating his frozen, infected fingers with a razor.

Malnourished men, women and children finally finding a piece of bread only to take a bite and find their teeth breaking off, falling down like crumbs.

Orphans eating cattle feed.

People slowly starving to death, bellies bloated, limbs withering into spindles, eyes bulging out.

Corpses clogging muddy pathways. Survivors forming patrols to gather the dead and pray the Kaddish.

These are memories of Jana Werner, a 55-year-old University Heights woman. She survived the Holocaust. Now she is talking publicly about it for the first time.

This past week, she and 150 other Cleveland area Holocaust survivors joined 15,000 people at the American Gathering of Holocaust Survivors in Washington. They commemorated the death of six million European Jews, systematically slaughtered by the Nazi regime.

"Healing is a very slow process because we lost so much," said Werner, president for five years of the Kol-Israel Sisterhood, an organization of Holocaust survivors here. "We lost an awful lot."

She immigrated to Cleveland in 1949. She was twenty-one, married to Nathan Werner, who had outlived Poland's death camps. They didn't talk much about the Holocaust then because the crime — six million innocent people gassed, machine-gunned, beaten and starved — was nearly beyond belief.

"When we came here nobody believed us," she said. "Nobody. Even American Jews. It's impossible to believe what we went through. They just couldn't believe that people can live through such inhumanity for such a long a time and come out and still be human beings."

Before the war, in her city of Chernovtsy, then in Romania's Bucovina province, Jana Werner lived among 100,000 Jews. In 1941, at thirteen, she and her parents and all other Jews were herded into cattle trains and shipped to the Ukraine's Transnistria province, the site of a huge slave labor camp and a depot for mass murder. In all, 200,000 Romanian Jews died in Transnistria before it was liberated in 1944.

"Their system of exterminating us was not through ovens," Werner said yesterday. "It was through dirt. Through filth. There was no soap, no clothes. People were naked. They didn't have food. So it was a miracle we came out alive there, that we came out normal people, that we have a population."

The trip to Washington rekindled her girlhood memories. Like many other Holocaust survivors, Werner wants us to learn her history, which is really our history, too.

Like many others, Werner believes that resurrecting the awful past can ensure the safety of the future; the most powerful deterrent to a new holocaust is the memory of the one that took place.

It's frightening, but the memory is fading for some. It has been only thirty-eight years since Hitler's demise, but already such groups as the Institute for Historical Review, composed of ultra-conservative scholars, insist that the Holocaust never really happened; that it's a Zionist hoax.

According to a U.S. opinion poll, a big group (40 percent) is "tired of Jewish concerns about the Holocaust."

In Europe, violence against Jews is escalating. Cemeteries in London are desecrated. Jews are targets of bombings in Ireland, Italy, West Germany and Austria.

"They think when you kill a Jew it doesn't hurt," Werner said. "It does hurt. When we cut our finger, we hurt. We bleed just like other people. When we lose somebody, we mourn. We still mourn those six million people."

Werner remembers walking into a ghost town on the Dniester River near the Russian border. She and the other Romanian Jews were being herded toward Transnistria and were stopping for awhile.

The houses had been ransacked. Windows were broken and doors smashed. Amid the ruin stood a temple. Inside, they found a message in Hebrew scrawled on a wall. It had been written by one of the city's last survivors.

It said: All the Jews in the city have been slain. If you understand this message, please say the Kaddish for us.

She stood and listened as twelve of the men with her put on black skullcaps and recited the Kaddish, the prayer for the dead.

"As long as we live, we always remember," Jana Werner said yesterday. "We must."

April 13, 1983

A thankless task

He took the jet from Santa Fe, New Mexico, with a goal in mind: *I'm gonna rob a store.*

He wanted money to finish his senior year at the University of New Mexico. So he thumbed through an atlas to pick a target. *I've never been to Ohio. I'll hit Ohio,* he thought.

A few hours later, at a Big Bear store in Columbus, Russell S. Sommers handed a man in the office a note: "Give me all the money and no one will get hurt."

Twenty minutes later, police found Sommers walking down a street. They found $1,038 stuffed in his pockets and arrested him. He ended up serving forty-five months in the state penitentiary in Marion.

One day recently, Sommers found himself in the back of a Cleveland Heights police car. They were zipping him off to the station.

The day had started out like every other weekday for Sommers, who is thirty-five and looking for work. He walked down to Caroll Drug on Coventry Road and bought a *Wall Street Journal.* He strolled up the street to Arabica, the coffee house, bought a cup of tea and took it and the newspaper to the back table he favors. While his tea steeped, he entered one of the two unisex washrooms.

Sitting on the back of the commode was a thick brown unmarked envelope.

Someone left his school papers, he thought. *I'll leave it at the register.*

Sommers opened the unsealed envelope in the privacy of the tiny washroom. He was flabbergasted. Neatly stacked and bound in rubber bands were six bundles of bills. He flipped through two bundles — ones, fives, tens and twenties, in no particular order. *Hell, put it under my arm and walk out,* he thought. The idea quickly faded. Sommers had a better idea.

He went to the store manager, Judy Natko, and asked if it was the store's money. She said, "No, let's call the police." He said, "Fine."

That's how he found himself sitting in the cruiser.

A 30-year-old woman showed up at the police station to claim the money. She knew how it was wrapped and exactly how much was in the envelope.

She said her name was Marilyn J. Kerins. She said the money was the take from four days of raising money for the Unification Church.

She didn't explain why she had left the cash in the washroom.

The church is run by the Rev. Sun Myung Moon, the convicted tax evader. Moon was found guilty of filing false tax returns, conspiring to evade taxes on $112,000 in interest income and failing to report $50,000 in shares received from an import company.

Because Sommers didn't fail to report or conspire to evade returning the money he found, Moon's empire will be $1,330 better off.

"I had law-abiding friends all around me shake their heads and say I'm a fool for what I did," Sommers said. "I don't agree with them. . . . I had just got off parole and I was proud of that. I had just gone out and registered to vote."

He is determined to go straight this time. "I haven't even got a parking ticket," he said. "In Cleveland Heights, that's saying a lot."

Sommers said the police told him the woman wasn't interested in thanking him for being honest.

"They said she told them I was just doing what I was supposed to do," Sommers said. "I don't want a reward. I'd like to be thanked."

"Russell did an honorable thing," said Cleveland Heights Police Chief Martin G. Lentz. The chief was told that the Moonie hadn't thanked Sommers.

"Would he settle for an autographed picture of Rev. Sun Myung Moon?" the chief joked.

For a few seconds, that cash had tempted a guy who's trying to stay straight.

"I wouldn't have been human if I hadn't thought about keeping it," Sommers said. "But I'm in a different frame of mind. I used to be out for the quick score. Now I'm concerned about what's best for me in the long run.

"I felt good. I wanted Arabica's respect for turning it in. I wanted the police's respect."

But you're not getting any respect from the people you helped.

"If I had to do it all over again with what I know now," said Sommers, who paused and took a deep breath, "I'd still do the same thing."

October 20, 1983

In the dark

Dennis Gibbons, the product of suburban schools, makes more than $25,000 a year stacking, bundling and inserting advertising sections into *The Plain Dealer*. He's what's known in the trade as a mailer.

You might think Gibbons, thirty-one, lives a good life. He recently bought a modest condominium in Avon Lake. He goes fishing on his boat. He's going to get married soon for the first time.

But Gibbons has a problem. You can't figure it out by looking at him or at his tax return.

He can't read the newspaper he helps put out. Nor can he write. He's illiterate.

"It's still a mystery," Gibbons was saying yesterday over the clacking whirl of the mailing room. "At first they thought it was dyslexia. I moved from different schools in Westlake, Rocky River, Fairview, North Olmsted. They'd try for a week or two, then pass me on. With fifty people in the class, one person couldn't get too much attention. After a while, I was just being passed from one grade to the next."

Gibbons, a tall, dark-haired man with a mustache, was taking a break from his spot on one of the whirlybirds, a carousel-like contraption that stuffs comics and advertising sections into the newspaper.

You may recall Gibbon's name. He was the guy who saved several children's lives in 1976 when he pulled them from a burning bus in Berea.

His dad had been a mailer at *The Cleveland Press* and got him into the union five years ago. Gibbons didn't even have to fill out a job application. The union trained him to work the whirlybird and the stacker and the forklift.

People are shocked to learn he can't even read a comic strip. "Their mouths will fly open," said Gibbons, who speaks with a stutter. "They ask me questions: 'Were you dropped on the head?' 'Are you kidding me?' They don't want to believe it. They don't think it's possible."

Today, on National Literacy Day, attention focuses on the 40,000 illiterates in the Cleveland area and 23 million nationwide.

Gibbons is lucky. The average illiterate makes half of what a high school graduate earns. If you can't read, the odds skyrocket that you'll end up on welfare or turn to crime.

If you can't read, you can't use the phone book to get help. You can't read warning labels on poisons or safety instructions at work. You can't shop for a bargain. You lose all around.

Gibbons also is lucky because he hooked up with Project: LEARN, a voluntary adult reading program at 2238 Euclid Avenue. Adults who can't read are tested, then given instruction books and two hours of private tutoring a week — free.

This spring, Gibbons was paired with a tutor, Jane West, who instructs him at her home. On August 9, he finished the thirteenth lesson, took the test and passed with a 94 percent. He made a few mistakes, writing *caq* for cup and misspelling Ed as *ei*.

He now can read *man, Mr., number, shop, snake, street, yes, you, zipper* and 130 other words — first grade level. That's just the beginning.

"Their lives don't get better in three months or six months," said Nancy Oakley, the dedicated director of Project: LEARN. "Maybe they've gone from first grade to fifth grade in reading, but they're still no more employable on the street. The puzzle is that there is still motivation."

Dennis Gibbons has kept himself motivated. A couple of people at work call him "retard" or "dummy." But, actually, he's clever. He was a diesel mechanic, learning the trade from memorizing diagrams. He can find his way around town by navigating from landmark to landmark. Looking for something in a drugstore, he'll say: "Excuse me, I forgot my glasses. Can you point out the aspirin to me?"

One of the first things he does every morning on the job is look for new notices that have been posted. He asks someone what they say. Someone also tells him the work schedule assigning him to what machine.

"You try to be like anybody else," Gibbons was saying. "You try not to let things bother you. I'm not bitter. When I was in school, teachers weren't trained to handle problems like mine."

A supervisor strolled by with a clipboard and told Gibbons he'd have to get back to the whirlybird.

"I've got a goal," Gibbon said, wrapping it up. "This job won't be here for the rest of my life. Automation is slipping in. I may not have a job in five, ten years. I'd like to join the Highway Patrol. Lotta people in the world need help. A lotta people have helped me. I'd like to return the favor."

September 8, 1983

Crime stopper

Some old ladies at the Riverview housing project on W. 25th Street won't leave their apartments.

They're afraid to step into hallways and elevators, let alone venture outdoors. They're scared that young thieves in the neighborhood will knock them down and snatch their purses or beat them for sport.

So they get on the phone and make an appointment with Noah Thomas.

Noah's their man. He will escort them across the street to the bank. He'll walk them a block to the West Side Market. He'll listen to their troubles. He understands.

Noah Thomas is an unlikely hero. He is seventy-three, stands 5-feet-6 and weighs 132 pounds. He's lived in public housing since 1976.

When Thomas pulls on the black and gray uniform of the Cleveland Police Auxiliary and covers his white hair with a patrolman's hat, he looks perhaps a decade younger.

But he's still slight. He has had four heart attacks and doesn't move too fast. He speaks softly and carries a walkie-talkie.

But Thomas is a crime stopper. Sometimes the uniform is all it takes.

"I've busted up a few crimes," he said modestly.

The other night, he was patroling at the West Boulevard Estates, a Cuyahoga Metropolitan Housing Authority high-rise for the elderly at 9520 Detroit Avenue, where he lives.

He encountered two thieves trying to hotwire a station wagon in the parking lot. They bolted. They weren't going to wait around and find out that the old man in uniform wasn't packing anything more deadly than a whistle and his pride.

At a time when many Cleveland residents are practically paralyz-ed by fear of crime, Thomas is acting. He is one of the more than five hundred in the Cleveland Police Auxiliary who volunteer their time to make things safer for the rest of us.

It's a full-time responsibility. Thomas has been working 2 a.m. to 4 a.m. lately, seven nights a week. During the daylight hours, he patrols three four-hour shifts a week.

His escorting at Riverview, where he had lived for four years, is his own doing. He climbs into his 1973 Plymouth Satellite and makes his rounds nearly every day.

"I just hate crime that much," said Thomas, sitting in the crowded common room at the high-rise one morning. "Some of the elderly people are afraid to go outside their door. They won't go outside until I get there."

Some don't go outside because they're handicapped. One woman in his building is crippled. She gets around, several inches a minute, with a four-legged walker.

Once a week, Thomas helps her into his car and takes her shop-ping. Without his help, she'd live out her life inside four walls.

John Dellasandro and Carol Guido, members of the Cleveland Police Department's community-response unit, know Thomas. Off duty, they work at the Sears store on W. 110th Street and Lorain Avenue where they sometimes see Thomas escorting the crippled lady into the store.

"It must take him four hours to get her into the store and back," Dellasandro remarked. "He's really something else."

Thomas isn't paid a dollar. He wouldn't take it anyway.

"The way I was brought up, my mother had a pattern," Thomas explained. "You had to do something before you sat down to eat, even if it was bringing in a handful of wood. I was always doing something.

"You see, some people are so selfish. They don't realize that if you help people without thinking of yourself, it comes back to you. Someone notices whenever you do good."

Thomas was three when his father died. His mother reared him and his four siblings in Jasper County, Georgia.

Young Noah always knew work. At fifteen, he was caddying at an Atlanta country club. For three years, he carried the clubs for golf great Bobby Jones.

In 1929, Thomas followed his older brother to Cleveland. He caddied at Canterbury Country Club for several years. He was a machinist at Ferro Corp. for eleven years. Then he worked at Ford

Motor Company for seventeen years before retiring in 1971.

All along, he toiled at one or two outside jobs, supporting his five kids and a wife who developed health problems and died in her fifties. At one time, he had a crew of five who did landscaping and lawn work at the big homes in Shaker Heights.

Thomas is proud of his work. "There wasn't one purse snatching on a payday," he said about the four years he patroled with his friends in the Adam-6 auxiliary unit at the Riverview projects.

When he moved into the West Boulevard Estates in November 1981, he had to talk its management into letting him start a patrol team there.

Now his neighbors come up to him and say: "Don't you move, Noah. We don't know what we'd do without you."

"All these people," said Thomas, looking around the room with a grin, "they're crazy about me."

March 21, 1983

Death of a legend

The woman at the maitre d's station was talking into the telephone.

"Yes, a few more weeks," she said pleasantly. "Yes, uh-huh. How many in your party? OK, fine. Thank you."

She hung up the phone. "Everybody is calling," the woman, Irene Gelety, said with a sigh. "They want to come in one last time before it closes."

Fourteen years she has worked at the Blue Fox restaurant. Fourteen great years and it's all over. Bruno has sold the place. He had a heart attack and sold it to one of those soulless restaurant chains. In a few weeks, one of the city's classic nightspots and fine restaurants will be gone.

The Blue Fox. If the restaurant were a singer, it would be Sinatra crooning "My Way." If a meal, it would be veal piccata, paper-thin. A car — Cadillac Eldorado, of course.

What will people remember? Autographed pictures from Frank and Dean and Bob Hope on the wall. Judge Frank Battisti eating dinner, his bodyguards at the ready. With his suit-and-tie crowd, Art Modell sitting across the room from Nick Mileti in jeans and tennis shoes, never exchanging a word. Earl Weaver and his bunch, getting loud, staying all night.

Who will share the memories? Politicians, judges, millionaires, monsignors, gamblers, bookies, FBI agents, car dealers, the crowd from the track, the crowd with the boats, and, mostly, ordinary folks.

When Bruno Berardinelli and Nate Buchantz opened the place on Clifton Boulevard sixteen years ago, it was like putting a piece of Short Vincent Street in Lakewood.

The last vestige of Short Vincent's old-fashioned Broadway

scene died when they buried the Theatrical's Mushy Wexler.

"The Fox was the only action place after that," said Ed Stinn, the car dealer.

It is Saturday night. The parking lot is packed with Cadillacs and Lincolns and station wagons. Inside, moving from table to table, is a sharply dressed, older man with thick, black eyebrows and a deep, expressive voice.

It's Bruno, the straw that stirs the drink. He's working the bar crowd now.

"Hi buddy," he said to a guy he doesn't know. He moved from one stool to the next, to the next. "Hi buddy, hi buddy, hi buddy."

Bruno's in the restaurant now. The strings of Tivoli lights are glimmering. The booths and upholstered chairs are occupied. Smoke rises, glasses clink, the place buzzes with talk and laughter. Vince in on the piano, singing "For the Good Times."

Bruno shakes another hand, rubs another guy's back. "How are ya, sweetie?" he asked a pretty woman in a summer dress. "You are a good-looking gal.

"We had the heavy hitters here last night," Bruno said after sitting down at a table and pouring himself a small glass of white wine. He names a few: Dick Jacobs, Dom Visconsi, Sam Miller.

One of the younger patrons asked Bruno what he's going to do. "I don't know," he said. "I'm gonna take it easy. I got a place in Florida."

He's got his real estate and warehouses in Bedford. "Still have my broker's license, but I never use it," he said.

Another restaurant? "Maybe, but don't tell my wife. She'll kill me. I'm supposed to be taking it easy."

Bruno has another thing on his mind. He was charged in March with possessing draw poker machines. The Blue Fox had a reputation of being a hangout for a few shady characters; this was part of its atmosphere. So were the FBI agents taking down license plate numbers in the parking lot.

In December, a bartender was arrested for taking sports bets at the bar. Joe Spaganlo, a regular customer and an alleged big bookmaker, was busted, too.

"I'm friendly to everybody," Bruno said. "If some FBI guy sees me friendly with so-called characters, I can't help it."

He's put up with the agents for years. "If I've done anything wrong, I'd be in jail," he said.

Once FBI agents came in and told Bruno they wanted to search the basement for evidence of gambling. "Better get a shovel," Bruno said. The restaurant doesn't have a basement.

At the end of World War II, while still in the service, Bruno met Buchantz. They opened the Blue Grass restaurant in Northfield. They made their money by relying on personal service and using the freshest ingredients in their food.

Later, they moved this winning formula to the West Side with the Blue Fox. It worked. Bruno is a rich man.

As long as there's a Las Vegas, as long as men wear pinkie rings, as long as people want to rub shoulders with the famous and the infamous, there will be a need for a Blue Fox.

But, Stinn said, "If Bruno said he'd keep it and not show up, it would die on the vine."

Norm Shibley, the lawyer and gourmand, has an omelette named after him on the Blue Fox after-theater menu.

"Without him center stage, it wouldn't do as well," he said. "He knew everybody, and those he didn't, he made a point to know. Bruno is one of a kind."

July 16, 1984

The dance of life

Benny's legs poked out of the white hospital gown. There, tattooed on his feet and shins, were the wages of his profession: Flat feet. Rough calloused toes. Thick, gnarled toenails. Dark scar tissue on his shins.

"We had steel taps on the heels and the toes," Benny said yesterday. "If you hit yourself dancing, you'd sure feel it."

Benny's real name is John Tetkowski. But most people know him by his stage name, Benny. From the 1930s to the 1950s, he tap-danced in nearly every nightclub and variety house and after-hours joint in town. Now, at sixty-four, he's fighting off pneumonia and a mild heart attack at St. John Hospital.

"I'm gonna pull out of it," he said. "Then I'm gonna behave myself. I'm not gonna dance too much."

Vaudeville has gone the way of the streetcar, and Benny, who never married, is left with memories:

Al Jolson giving him tips on how to sing Dixieland.

Working with Bud Abbott and Lou Costello, Jimmy Durante and Gypsy Rose Lee.

Benny tap-dancing at the Roxy Theater, sandwiched between the chorus girls and the comedians. Benny gliding out on stage, jangling his feet to the music, firing a one-liner, then into a song-and-dance sketch.

Benny singing "Swanee" and "Rockabye My Baby to a Dixie Melody," dancing all the while, working in a joke, then jumping behind the bar and playing the whiskey bottles with spoons.

"I picked that up myself by watching other guys," Benny said. "If you wasn't a buck-and-wing dancer, a tap dancer, if you didn't pick it up, you weren't one of the boys. You couldn't hang around with them guys."

It was the Depression and "them guys" were the entertainers, the guys who could walk into a bar empty-handed and come out with pockets stuffed with silver.

Benny was a young guy working in an after-hours joint as a doorman and dice table operator.

"I worked for the Shadowland, then the Mickey Mouse Club," he said. "Everybody who was in show business would go there. They'd all get up on the stage and do something. It was always a riot. The cops would come to break in the joint, and everybody would run out the back door."

While his Polish buddies were settling down at the steel mills and factories, Benny was learning the ropes of a different trade: you always make friends with the piano player and the drummer. Everybody else in the band follows these two. If they don't like you, they can make you look like a bum. Also, when you dance in a bar, have a shill, someone to throw a dollar bill on the floor near the end of your routine, so the customers get the idea and follow suit.

In the 1960s, Benny called it quits. Business was lousy. The Roxy closed. People were watching TVs. He worked as a cashier in a state liquor store for five years, tap-dancing occasionally at the Flat Iron Cafe.

"I have never regretted it," Benny said. "Everybody in show business I ever had contact with I loved."

Most of his buddies are gone, but once a month Benny remembers them. He takes a bus to St. John's Cathedral and lights a candle for the buskers and bookies and barmaids who once inhabited Short Vincent and E. 9th Street and E. 105th Street. He gives them a final applause.

From a wallet, Benny pulled a stack of death notices and passed them over to a visitor.

"Anybody who ever died in show business, we had a habit," he said. "We put a dime in a candle and lit it for someone who died in vaudeville or show business."

The talk was getting serious. Benny knows about pacing a show, so he switched the subject.

"I was at Moe's Main Street on 79th," he said, chuckling. "Johnny Ray was playing there. I was drunk and he was singing that song, 'Cry.' Tears were coming down his face. I went in the kitchen and came back with sledgehammer and broke the piano. They said, 'What are you doing?' I said, 'I couldn't stand him singing that song, I don't like an entertainer crying.' I had to sing two months for Moe to pay it off."

A nurse rushed into the hospital room. During the conversation, Benny had accidentally knocked out one of the wires from the tiny heart monitor attached to his chest. The big monitor down the hall told the nurse Benny was dead: no heartbeat, just a flat line on a TV screen.

But Benny wasn't dead. The nurse found him sitting up, wishing his fingers were curled around a big cigar and a tumbler of whiskey.

"I thought I'd get out of here tomorrow," Benny went on. "Now they tell me I have to stay another week. I wanted to get outta here, go to a couple parties. I had a chance to make a couple of bucks. This Thanksgiving I could make fifty bucks at one party. I was gonna take a chance. After the party, I got my fifty bucks, then I wouldn't dance for a couple weeks. You know, take it easy."

November 15, 1983

A bike for Danny

She bought it for one dollar at a garage sale. It was a big, battered old-fashioned tricycle that needed three new wheels.

Not a bad deal, Karen Filkins thought. This will be perfect for my Danny.

Danny is ten years old and retarded. He cannot talk. Filkins and her husband, Dan, live on the West Side.

She took her son and the tricycle to Farrell's Bike Shop, 6699 Eastland Road, in suburban Middleburg Heights.

From the road, it's hard to believe Farrell's is the biggest bike repair shop in the area. It looks like a shack surrounded by trash. The shop is a small building set forty yards from the road. It's surrounded by stacks of wood pallets and piles of scrap steel and empty five-gallon cans. A couple of dogs roam the yard.

Inside the shop are jumbles of bike parts: inner tubes, rims, sprockets, handle bars and frames. Hanging from the ceiling are new spoked rims and tires. Cats wander among the merchandise.

Standing behind the workbench is Tom Farrell, a 75-year-old Irishman in a baseball cap and work clothes. Farrell is a short, broad-shouldered man with a plump middle. He could pass for sixty-five. He and his wife, Mary, live in Brook Park.

"I haven't been to a doctor since 1942 when I went in the service," he said. "I haven't taken an aspirin in my life. My dad was the same way. He died at ninety-three."

When Karen Filkins brought in the old bike and her son, Farrell smiled and said, "Sure, I'll fix it up."

A few weeks later, she picked up the tricycle. It looked new. Farrell had driven to Pennsylvania to get the wheels for Danny's bike. After he showed it to Danny, the boy said, "Thank you," in sign language.

"Can he hear?" Farrell asked Danny's mom.

When she said yes, Farrell went to a drawer and pulled out a shiny bell and attached it to the handlebars.

Danny climbed on the bike and began ringing and ringing the bell.

Karen Filkins and Farrell got the bike and Danny into the car. He was waving goodbye when his mother tried to pay Farrell.

"I turned to pay him," she said, "but he just walked away and said, 'No, no, go on home and let him enjoy it.' I had tears in my eyes and said thanks again.

"I thought, God bless you for making my Danny's life a little brighter."

Yesterday, as is his custom, Farrell was working.

"I'm seventy-five," he said. "What am I going to do on Sunday, sit and watch TV?"

He was listening to a ball game on TV and cleaning some spokes. Spring is a busy time for bike repair.

"Sure, I take care of crippled people as much as I can," he said, answering a visitor's question. "People bring their wheelchairs in here to be fixed. We don't charge them."

He began fixing bikes in the early 1930s and later set up a shop on W. 25th Street near Queen Avenue.

A metallurgist by training, Farrell worked for Midland Steel Co. About four decades ago, the year his son, John, graduated from high school, Farrell quit.

With slowdowns and strikes, he wasn't making enough to put John through college. So Farrell told his boss he was opening a salvage scrap metal business on Eastland Road. His boss told him he was crazy.

But Farrell prospered, and his son went to college.

Farrell pulled a business card from his wallet yesterday. It was grimy and frayed from handling. It said, "John J. Farrell, Chairman of the Department of Chemistry, Franklin and Marshall College, Lancaster, Pennsylvania."

Farrell, proud and independent, runs his business on trust. Only three people have bounced checks at the bike shop over the decades.

Business sense seems to run in the Farrell family. His mother owned a general store in Bob's Run, West Virginia. His brother runs a thriving floral business in Columbus. His 84-year-old sister has a bakery in Pittsburgh.

"You just don't want another guy telling you what to do," said

Farrell, explaining his motivation. "Here's the thing: If any one of my kids wanted to go down to see the Indians, I could always hang a sign on the door and go. If I was working at Ford or Midland, I couldn't ring out."

April 11, 1983

Dream City

Some colleagues smashed up on booze. Other committed suicide. Work finally took its toll; Hank Richardson was burned out.

Since the late 1960s, he had designed bombs for big Pentagon contractors. The money was great but the pressure was murder. He worked 18-hour days. His first marriage cracked up. He began doubting the value of his work. *This stuff may end up wiping out the planet.*

This spring, Hank did what many people dream about. He took off for a year. He left his job in Tampa, Florida. He took his wife and $20,000 and moved away.

"I got lucky with a couple of minor investments," he explained. "I always wanted to take a year off. People always talk about taking off to write a book or whatever, and they never do it. I wanted to do it."

His break from work didn't surprise friends. The city he moved to did.

Hank is forty-two and bears a striking resemblance to comedian Jerry Lewis. With a Ph.D. in physics, Hank is a scientific thinker. He and his wife of four years, Kathy, twenty-five, used a systematic approach to figure in what city to enjoy their one-year sabbatical.

They got road maps and a *World Almanac* and made a list of major cities, with such headings as *Food, Health Care, Entertainment, Weather, Population* and so on. They were working with a $1,500-a-month budget, so they crossed New York and Los Angeles off the list.

They wanted to live where the seasons changed. They needed a city with a health insurance policy group they could join. They wanted a place with a variety of ethnic foods, movies and plays.

They hit the road, visiting Boston, Columbus, Louisville, Nashville, Houston, Minneapolis, Philadelphia, even Erie, Pennsylvania. They bought local newspapers, checked the entertainment listings, read the classified ads line-by-line, made notes and impressions.

They found their city: Cleveland.

"It surprised me when I looked at it on paper," Kathy Richardson said. It had everything they wanted but cable TV.

Their friends were surprised. Their remarks ran something like: "You're taking a year off, you can live anywhere you want, and you're moving to . . . Cleveland? Sure you are. C'mon, what's the punchline?"

No joke. Hank and Kathy Richardson live on the top floor of a big restored brick home on Franklin Boulevard just west of Ohio City.

They jog through the city's neighborhoods. They go to concerts at Blossom. They browse the antique stores on Lorain Avenue. They buy groceries at the West Side Market. Hank works on a mystery novel. Kathy is training for a marathon. They say they love Cleveland. They can't believe people put it down.

"People don't realize how much Cleveland has compared to other cities," Hank said. "The average guy on the street thinks of it as an outhouse. Cleveland has been the butt of jokes. People think of it as a working man's dump. [Yet] Cleveland has such a nice gentle roll to it. It's a big city, but people are gentle, friendly."

Hank and Kathy know Cleveland geography better than most natives. They run nearly an hour a day through the neighborhoods. Hank has lost twenty pounds of fat since he moved here. His blood pressure dropped from 140 over 90 to 110 over 70. Kathy has built up her speed and endurance.

"I like your bridges," she said. "I like your river and the traffic."

"I can walk into Cleveland Clinic and get attention," Hank continued. "I can't walk in the Einstein School of Medicine in New York unless I come in a limo. I had to wait six weeks to see a dental expert here. I'd have to wait six months in New York, if I got an appointment at all."

"It's not too formal," Kathy said. "You can go almost anywhere without a tie on."

"We've been through the Ford plant and U.S. Steel," Hank said. "We'd like to ride one of the ore boats."

"We went to the Air Show," Kathy said. "We really enjoyed it.

There's so much to do here."

When the money runs out, the Richardsons will probably return to Tampa where Hank will toil as a nuclear physicist. Unless he can make some money on his thriller.

"It's about a scientist who gets caught up in a government sponsored plot to control people," Hank said. "It's about how this guy comes out from the shroud he was under and destroys the work he accomplished and finds trouble doing that."

For a sequel, he could write about a couple who make a strange move to a much maligned Midwest city and find happiness.

September 5, 1983

Forever Peter Pan

He had it all: a stunning wife, devoted friends, two successful record stores, a national reputation in his field, expensive playthings.

Peter T. Schliewen also possessed a rare commodity — what his friends called "style."

He grew his hair long before it was fashionable. He was the first to cut it short. He always had the best seats at the hottest rock concerts. He helped "break" rock star David Bowie in Cleveland a decade ago and got a gold record for his efforts.

"The Catalog of Cool" says Schliewen's Record Revolution on Coventry Road is the "coolest place to buy records" in Ohio. Rock 'n' roll's big names have been there to shop and sign their autographs on the wall: Bruce Springsteen, The Who, Elvis Costello, Led Zeppelin, Southside Johnny, Lou Reed, Patti Smith, Mott the Hoople and many more.

Always in control, never intimidated, Schliewen could walk into any situation, talk to anyone. But it's all over now.

Last Thursday, Schliewen joined friends at Nighttown's annual Bloomsday party. It was a warm, peaceful night. As usual, he was dressed in tight, pressed blue jeans and a $65 Italian sport shirt. With bright blue eyes, blond hair and handsome, vulnerable looks, he reminded friends of an older James Dean.

A few hours and drinks later, Schliewen left with an acquaintance and climbed into his black Porsche 911SC and roared off. He was an excellent driver who loved to move fast. "How would you like to go on the ride of a lifetime?" he would ask his friends.

About 11 p.m., traveling at terrific speed on Shaker Boulevard, the car apparently spun out, skidded, jumped a curb and wrapped around a tree.

Schliewen and his passenger, Tracey Adams, twenty-five, were thrown from the wreck. She lies unconscious in Suburban Hospital with a fractured hip and arm. He died of multiple rib fractures, internal bleeding and lacerations of the lungs. He was forty-one.

"He lived fast, died young and left a beautiful corpse," said David Roth, a friend. "He was always riding around with a James Dean head on his shoulders. . . . If there was a way Peter chose to go, it would be in a blaze of glory, doing life in the fast lane."

Schliewen loved the thrill of high speed, but he also demanded control. So what happened? How did one side of his personality overwhelm the other?

"I've been here thirty-one years and never seen anything like this crash," said Shaker Heights Police Chief George Lamboy, whose department and the county coroner are still investigating. "There are so many unanswered questions."

Gathered at the funeral on Monday were bankers, bikers, millionaire friends and freaks. The popular reggae band, I-tal, played at the church.

Bob Roth, a pharmacist and Schliewen's closest friend, gave a eulogy. He mentioned a slogan that fit Peter: "He who dies with the most toys, wins."

That was Peter. He had a souped-up Jeep, a hot Porsche, a bored and stroked Harley Davidson XLS1000, even a souped-up Weedeater that he fed 100-octane aviation fuel.

"Peter liked to live on the edge," his second wife, Janna, twenty-eight, would say later. "He was so dashing, just like one of those old movie characters."

Despite the carefree image, he lived a life of routine. He ate the same breakfast, he always wore jeans, he hosed down the sidewalk of his Coventry store in the mornings after reading *The New York Times*. On Fridays, usually, he sat at Table 10 in Nighttown and had prime rib, never a salad, drinking Heineken beer.

He was fastidious. His cars were immaculate. He always took a car wherever he went. That way he could leave when he wanted. For someone in the rock industry, he was an average drug user. He smoked weed or snorted cocaine socially.

"Many people were jealous of him," Roth said yesterday. "He never grew old and lived a life they envied."

So why did he die?

"I don't know," Roth said. "He thought he was invulnerable behind the wheel. He seemed to know every bump and chuckhole in every street."

At the funeral, Schliewen's mother remarked that Peter was an apt name because her son was like Peter Pan: "He never wanted to grow old."

Janna Schliewen, his wife, agreed with the image.

"Peter Pan never grew up," Janna explained. "Peter Pan took people on trips and wonderful adventures and brought them back safely. That's what [my] Peter did."

Until last Thursday, when Schliewen, with what his friends called "style," put himself in Never Never Land and Tracey Adams in a hospital.

Janna said she had begged her husband to cut out the fast driving. "But," she sighed, "if he changed that, he wouldn't be Peter anymore."

June 23, 1983

Ghostly employee

A burly guy in silver hair and a rust suit was sitting on a bench outside a federal courtroom yesterday morning. The guy, Allen Friedman, sixty-two, is Jackie Presser's uncle.

Friedman was waiting for the verdict in his embezzlement trial. He was sitting next to his wife, Nancy, a smartly dressed woman in her late thirties with fashion-model cheekbones.

"I have a feeling it's *guilty*," he told his wife.

Soon it was announced that the jury had reached a verdict after five hours of deliberation over two days.

"I knew it the minute the jury walked in," Nancy Friedman said minutes later. "They wouldn't look at us. I knew it was *guilty*."

Allen Friedman: guilty on all four counts of embezzling Teamsters Union Local 507 funds by being a ghost employee, convicted of cashing eighty-nine paychecks worth $165,000 for doing no work over four years.

All the checks bore one of two signatures: that of Jackie Presser, now the Teamsters president, or that of Harold Friedman (no relation), Local 507 president.

Allen Friedman, the guy with a bad heart, was puffing on another cigarette. Jack Levin, his brash lawyer, was complaining about the verdict. Nancy Friedman, her eyes behind sunglasses, was shaking, trying to smoke a cigarette. They went down the courthouse elevator.

They reached the only exit and saw the TV cameras and reporters. "Let's not go out now," Nancy Friedman said.

"They're not going away," Levin told her. "And take the cigarette out of your mouth."

Allen Friedman walked down the steps. The reporters began firing questions about his nephew, boss of the world's biggest union.

A few months ago, Friedman told NBC-TV: "Jackie Presser should have been in jail dozens of times, going back thirty years. He thinks I won't testify against him . . . but I don't like the things he's done, double-crossing me, doing what he's doing to the working people. And I'll do whatever I have to."

Yesterday, Friedman had no comment. Levin the lawyer cut off the questions about Presser: "I don't know if Allen has anything to say about Jackie Presser."

Presser is the target of a Labor Department investigation into alleged ghost employees at his Local 507. Yesterday, Allen Friedman said he thought the government was trying to get Presser through him.

Friedman is five years older than his nephew. Friedman's parents died before he was fourteen. He then was reared by William and Faye Presser, parents of Jackie Presser.

Allen said he was like an older brother to Jackie, and taught Presser everything he knows about union organizing and about other matters. "Jackie couldn't find his way downtown," Allen Friedman said yesterday, smiling at a memory.

The Friedmans and their lawyers began walking to the federal probation office a few blocks away to pick up some forms.

"I will not take no government deal," Friedman declared. "Jails don't frighten me, OK? . . . I am not afraid of man nor beast nor jail, OK?"

"At least you'll get some rest," Nancy Friedman told her husband on the walk over.

"I'm not going to jail," he reassured her. "They'll have to put me in a hospital."

"What happens here?" Nancy Friedman asked when they reached the hall outside the probation office. Levin explained that a probation officer would make a pre-sentence report about the likelihood that Friedman would commit the crimes he was convicted of again.

"How's he gonna have an opportunity to commit a crime?" Levin told the reporter who accompanied them. "He's not even with a union."

"I didn't commit a crime," Friedman corrected.

"He didn't commit a crime," Levin told the reporter.

Friedman found a chair in the reception room. He sat calmly while his wife went off to call their two teen-age daughters.

"How long have I got to live?" asked Friedman, who has suffered two massive heart attacks. "The doctor gave me a year to live in 1976. They gave me a day in 1982. This is all just another chapter in my book."

When Nancy Friedman returned, her husband had disappeared into an inside room.

"He's so cool," she told a man sitting nearby. "That bothers me. He holds it inside. If he'd just said something."

Friedman was asked to say something. Will he talk to the government about his nephew?

He smiled and said: "It will all come out in the book."

They walked through the noontime rush on Superior Avenue to a parking lot to pick up Levin's black Cadillac and go to lunch.

"I just can't imagine that Jackie Presser and Harold Friedman are feeling comfortable now," Nancy Friedman said.

September 29, 1983

Making ends meet

She never thought she'd end up dancing in a topless bar.

Morgan, twenty-three, is a recent Kent State University graduate. She is bright, holds a degree in journalism and public relations, and has worked as a vending machine mechanic.

IBM interviewed her several times, but nothing worked out. She tried sales, everything, but still couldn't find a decent job. Her husband is a builder, which these days means he's usually unemployed and looking for work.

Things took a turn for the worse last winter. Morgan was finishing her degree while her husband bid on small construction jobs by day and parked cars at a restaurant by night.

She always had dreamed of being Mitzi Gaynor, so one night she and her husband decided they might make ends meet if she danced at the Crazy Horse Saloon, 1438 St. Clair Avenue.

When they went to the club the first night to check things out, Morgan discovered that three of her Heights High classmates were dancers.

"There's no way I could possibly do this," Morgan said at the time. "I'm too shy. I'm too modest."

She came next week for Amateur Night, won the second place $50 and her career was born. She chose Morgan as a stage name.

"It's a job," she said. "You've got to clock in, check out, report to the bosses, the customers are always right and you've got to wear nice clothes. It's a job. I'm hoping the economy will take a turn for the better. I don't want to be here for very long."

Yesterday afternoon, Morgan took the Crazy Horse stage in a thigh-high shift and black high heels. She swung around a fireman's pole and started moving her hips suggestively to the disco beat and flashing lights. Except for the music, this could have been a scene fifteen years ago at the old Hullabaloo dance club.

Then Morgan took off her shift. She was wearing nothing save a garter belt, purple bikini panties and two strategically placed surgical eye patches.

"The eye patches were my idea," she said later. "I got them at a medical supply store. Now all the girls wear them."

She danced and smiled, looked a couple of guys in the eye, lip-synching the song's lyrics. *I need you all night. I need you all right.*

She danced near the edge of the stage and one of the guys slipped a dollar bill into her garter and then she danced away.

Morgan is slender with waist-length, strawberry blond hair and pale blue eyes. With her oval face and long, graceful nose and perfect tiny teeth set in a smallish mouth, she resembles the actress Meryl Streep.

"I come from an old-fashioned European family," she said. "It was stricter for me than my brother. I was the girl. I was raised the right way. Clean living, honesty. They're good parents. That's one reason I can't tell them what I'm doing."

Morgan makes much more than a beginning reporter or public relations assistant. She said she pulls in about $500 a week — $100 in salary and the rest in tips. She dances six 20-minute stints in her 11 a.m. to 7 p.m. shift.

Morgan relies on her regulars, maybe fifteen customers who each are good for $20 in tips a week. "One man tips me $20 every time I dance," she said. "I know about his wife, his kids, where they go to school. I know what kind of cologne he likes. He's an older man, very nice."

For the $20, the nice older man gets a kiss on the cheek and a few minutes of conversation and, like everyone else in the bar, four songs worth of suggestive dancing and come-on smiles.

"I've learned how terribly lonely a married man can be," Morgan said. "I used to think if a married man came into a place like this, he should be condemned, horsewhipped. Not any more. I've learned to appreciate my husband more. I've learned to read his problems a little better. I know when something on his mind bothers him."

She uses her earnings to buy food and pay the rent. The rest is sunk into her husband's small building company.

"I do the paper work," she said. "He does mostly masonry work. He's doing the stucco on a small office building right now. He's built houses. He does carpentry. He does everything but electrical work."

Next week, Morgan will interview for a job with Wang Laboratories Inc., the computer maker.

"I hope I get it," she said. "I'd like to wear regular clothes."

July 8, 1982

Sleeping Beauty

She was eleven when she learned the terrible truth.

Venita Fratantonio was cleaning her family's Cleveland Heights home and came across a big envelope stuffed with yellowing newspaper clippings.

"Hush of Slumber Breaks a Mother's Heart," said a 1960 headline over a photograph of Venita at five years of age. Her three-year-old sister appeared in an adjacent photo over the caption, "A nurse coaxes Bernadette from sleep."

Venita sat transfixed for an hour, reading the headline and stories about her bizarre childhood: "Help Offers Pour in for Sleeping Beauties," "Empty Bottle Adds to 'Beauties' Puzzle," and finally, "Love Affair Guilt Held Motive in Drugging Girls."

The story of Cleveland's Sleeping Beauties captured reporters and readers worldwide. Newspapers across the nation wrenched every shred of sensationalism from the case of the cute, little girls "whose mystery ailment touched the nation's heart."

The real story began when Bernadette, three, daughter of Vincent and Lillian Fratantonio, was admitted to a hospital after drinking a bottle of hair tonic. After her stomach was pumped, she slept for hours, then days, waking only occasionally.

Doctors were stumped. They made many tests, but couldn't find a cause. She was sent to experts in New York City, without success. She was subjected to more than three hundred tests, including spinal taps, brain scans, bone marrow exams and liver biopsies.

"This is the most fabulous case I know of," said the Fratantonios' pediatrician at the time. "We have just about run out of ideas."

Ten months later, Venita came down with the weird sleeping

sickness and the story intensified.

"Money and gifts and prayers poured in from all over the nation to a case that seemed to be a family tragedy," said one account.

When Lillian Fratantonio, twenty-nine, was about to have another baby and unable to visit her girls, they stopped sleeping. This gave doctors a clue. The girls were tested for barbiturates.

Later, a *Plain Dealer* photographer, cooperating with police, took secret photos as the mother fed her daughters with a medicine dropper. Police recovered from her purse a dropper with traces of barbiturates. When shown the photos, she confessed.

Lillian Fratantonio has never explained why she drugged her girls. She was found guilty and served time in the Workhouse.

During her trial for child endangering, it came out that Lillian Fratantonio, who had worked in a Cleveland Heights drugstore, was having an affair with another worker.

Police Sgt. Norman Ferris, who investigated the case, theorized at the time: "The woman was suffering from a deep-seated guilt complex because of her infidelity. She felt a need to punish herself. Instead, she turned upon those she loved — her two daughters."

At twenty-eight, Venita Fratantonio, the older Sleeping Beauty, is a pretty, petite woman with long dark hair and sad, deep-set brown eyes. This weekend, she gave her first interview about her infamous childhood.

She told of reading the old clippings and asking her mom why she did it.

"She said, 'The past is over, and it's none of your business. Don't believe everything you read,'" Venita recalled.

Venita went to Ursuline Academy and got A's. She graduated, then worked as a waitress until late 1978. That's when she had surgery for bleeding ulcers.

Doctors removed part of her stomach. During the operation, they accidentally nicked her kidney. It became abscessed and doctors removed it.

She was in the hospital five months, taking Percodan for pain. She became addicted to the powerful painkiller. She thinks she was predisposed to become an addict because she was on drugs as a child.

For about two years after she left the hospital, Venita lied to various doctors to get Percodan. She would alter the prescriptions to obtain larger amounts. She was caught and convicted of a minor drug charge. In jail after her arrest, Venita was attacked by three inmates.

"That's when I started to quit [drugs]," Venita said. "I was scared."

She dried out at a Toledo drug rehabilitation center. "I went through hell," she said. "It was the hardest thing I had to do."

Now she wants to finish college and get involved in law enforcement, maybe as an investigator.

The other Sleeping Beauty, Bernadette, is married, has two children and lives in Virginia.

Venita is not bitter about the lousy hand life has dealt her.

"In fact, it gives me more incentive to go on," Venita explained. "Knowing that people make mistakes gives me incentive to try and make my own life right. It makes me want to make my life better, no matter what obstacles I have to overcome. My mother overcame. She's doing real well. She works in a toy store and sells insurance."

There is still one thing Venita would like: an explanation from her mom.

"If she just said, 'I made a mistake,' " Venita said. "I'd like to hear it from her some day."

June 20, 1983

Business drive

Otto Kaminsky is a 73-year-old inventor. He has patented a clever new watch. Now he is waiting for the world to beat a path to his Maple Heights door.

When customers get there, they will probably be buying watches bearing the words, "Made in Japan."

Kaminsky has tried and tried to interest American manufacturers in his invention. It's a bowler's watch with a bezel (movable rim) that will indicate to a bowler where to stand and how to throw the ball to make a spare for any of the 1,023 different pin combinations.

Kaminsky knows the watch will sell because he knows bowling and its market. He has bowled a 725 series and a 286 game. At sixteen, he founded a bowling league and is still active in leagues, of which Greater Cleveland has 2,200.

So he wrote to a dozen different U.S. watchmakers. He asked about prices and requirements the manufacturers would need to churn out the watches for Kaminsky's company, Modek Enterprises. No replies.

"I'm just wondering who's minding the store," Kaminsky said angrily. "With this country's perilous economic climate, I'm wondering why people aren't interested in business. Nobody seems to care. Nobody is minding the store. Nobody's interested in following up on leads."

Nobody, except the Japanese watchmakers he contacted.

"The Japanese, they're the ones who responded in total," Kaminsky said. "They sent me a complete rundown on everything I need. When I write them, they'll answer promptly and in detail. That shows the kind of good businessmen they are. We can take a lesson from them."

U.S. watchmakers were not the only ones who didn't respond to Kaminsky's business proposition. Plastic molding companies and printing companies didn't answer his inquiries either.

"I find it so difficult to get responses, to get off the ground, to get the things I desperately need to get going," Kaminsky said. "I think we lack the enthusiasm, the appetite for business, the enthusiasm for work, for detail. You've got to have that.

"The Japanese, they're good businessmen, no question about it. They used to be the world's worst businessmen. They made a lot of mistakes. Now they seem to be the very best. They have the know-how. They have the enthusiasm."

In the face of adversity, it's a wonder small businessmen like Otto Kaminsky keep on plugging.

But he is in good company. Polaroid (instant photographs), Xerox (dry-process photocopying) and Sony (the transistor radio) were all small and unknown companies that offered their new ideas to big corporations, only to be turned down.

Then there is President Reagan who, when he deigns to speak about the economy, gives Kaminsky and those like him a rhetorical pat on the back.

But the President's economic policies — certainly, his high-interest money policy — punish small business while rewarding big business with tax write-offs.

It's guys like Kaminsky who should be rewarded with weighted tax cuts and low-interest loans. Consider their achievements:

Two-thirds of all new jobs in the private sector since 1976 were created by businesses with twenty or fewer employees.

Between 1953 and 1973, small businesses developed half the major innovations and twenty-four times as many break-throughs per research dollar as their big business counterparts.

Of the three big steel-making break-throughs — Bessemer, open-hearth and basic oxygen furnace — the U.S. steel industry developed none. A sculptor invented the ballpoint pen, an undertaker the dial telephone, and the list goes on.

And as long as human beings come equipped with brains, hands and backbones, some of us, guys like Otto Kaminsky, will use these gifts to challenge the marketplace. The just desert is not only a payoff someday, but the immediate sweet satisfaction of labor.

"I'm not that discouraged," Kaminsky said. "I'm gonna get it off the ground."

July 19, 1982

Blockbuster story

The life of a big city newspaper columnist is rarely boring. At any moment, you could be called upon to cover some earth-shaking event that changes the course of civilization.

Just the other day, I thought I had my hands on such a story. It started with a phone call from a stranger.

Reporters receive lots of calls from strangers. They say amazing things. One might claim to be a long-lost third cousin of Howard Hughes. Another could profess to have the goods on a crooked mayor. You get a lot of callers saying such things as, "The FBI is bugging my phone because the CIA needs its help trying to kill me."

Most of the time, these calls are rumor, speculation or fantasy, but they must be listened to and checked out. You never know when a phone tip will lead to a great story.

As I was saying, I got a call. A man named Arthur said he had a blockbuster for me: His cat could talk.

He said his cat, Mr. White, could say "hello," "yum, yum, yum," "love you," "groundhog," and twenty-two other words.

I told him I'd stop by to interview Mr. White.

In an easy chair in the den of a ranch-style home on Richmond Road sat Arthur. He was a huge, egg-shaped guy with big jowls and a pleasant voice tinged with a country twang.

Arthur, a retired salesman, had spread out on the carpet about sixty cassette tapes. The tapes recorded his conversations with Mr. White. Each tape bore a date and the word Mr. White supposedly said on the tape.

"Where's Mr. White?" I asked. "I'd like to talk to him."

Arthur explained that only he had ever handled Mr. White. The cat spoke only to him and, even then, only when he felt like it.

"But let me play you one of these tapes," Arthur said.

Arthur explained that he had rigged a microphone in Mr. White's giant cage in the garage. About forty feet of wire, strung from the house to the garage, connected the mike to a tape recorder next to the easy chair.

Arthur turned on the recorder. A live remote broadcast from the garage! We could hear Mr. White padding around the cage.

Arthur then picked a tape and slapped it into the recorder.

"Listen," he said. "Here's where he says hello."

The cat on the tape went, "Mee-oo."

Arthur picked another tape and said, "Here's where he says 'yum yum yum.' "

The cat on the tape went, "Mew mew mew."

Arthur was clearly excited. "Here he says, 'Love you.' You'll hear it."

The cat on the tape went, "Meow mew."

"I wanna hear him say 'groundhog,' " I demanded.

Arthur played another tape. I heard a recording of Arthur's voice: "say groundhog, Mr. White, groundhog. Groundhog."

The cat went, "Rrreow-oh."

"Of all the words in the dictionary, why do you think it says groundhog?" I asked.

Arthur explained that he grew up in Franklin County, Pennsylvania, during the Depression and that his father had been killed in a coal mine explosion.

"The only meat we ate back then was groundhog," Arthur said. "I'd go out and shoot 'em."

Arthur, who strums guitar and sings, played me a tape of a country song that went something like: "Groundhog, groundhog sitting on a log. Got me a shotgun and a yaller dog."

Arthur said he played the groundhog tape over and over again for Mr. White until the cat could say "groundhog."

I asked to see Mr. White.

In the garage, in a two-level cage covered with chicken wire and a sign that said "Mr. White's Condo," sat Mr. White. He was a beautiful, white-furred, long-haired cat.

"Talk to me, Mr. White," I said.

The cat just blinked.

"How are you today, Mr. White?"

Blink, blink.

I've got to quit wasting my time on these crazy phone tips, I thought. I told Arthur I was leaving.

"I take it you're not too convinced," he asked.

That's right.

"You're missing out on the story of your career. Scientists are gonna be out here studying him."

I said goodbye. End of story.

By the way, to the woman who called me about her yodeling field mouse, something has come up and I have to postpone our interview. Don't call me, I'll call you.

June 11, 1984

4

POLITICAL ANIMALS

It's only fair

The invoice looked like a shopping list for a small wrecking crew: two sledgehammers, a couple of three-foot crowbars, some staple guns, wire, screwdrivers, pliers.

It was a bill for "office supplies" for State Auditor Thomas E. Ferguson.

Ferguson, who oversees 900 people who audit the budgets and books of various state offices, is supposed to be Ohio's watchdog on government fraud and waste. Why would his office require a sledgehammer and a crowbar?

"Gee, I don't know," he said yesterday. "We do many things around the office. Maybe they needed them for something."

Maybe he needs the tools to pry secrets from former treasurer's department cashier Elizabeth Jane Boerger, the supposed amnesiac who can't remember what she did with $1.3 million of our state taxes.

Ferguson's office audited Boerger's operation in 1977 and 1978 but overlooked the missing money and instead gave the Treasurer's office a clean bill of health.

Most likely, the tools were used to put up tents at Ohio county fairs. County fairs are a state politician's bread and butter. Putting campaign workers at the fairs is one of the cheapest, most efficient ways to reach voters across the state.

Ferguson loves county fairs, and he has invoices to prove it. "Clean and repair three tents — $395," reads one invoice. "Wash four tents and one sidewall — $580," reads another. "Five vinyl banners — TOM FERGUSON, Ohio State Auditor — $422," reads a third.

Ferguson has a great thing going at the county fairs. He uses his employees to hand out his promotional literature on state time.

"The auditor's office did this under Jim Rhodes and under my father," Ferguson said. "It's like charging a congressman for using the mail [franking privileges] to put out literature."

Ferguson said he spent state money putting his workers at county fairs because the public needed to be educated about what his office does.

But a look at the literature shows just what kind of education Ferguson has in mind.

One leaflet talks about welfare fraud. Curiously enough, Ferguson has hammered alleged welfare fraud into his major issue in his re-election campaign against Vincent J. Campanella, Cuyahoga County commissioner.

Another leaflet displays a nice picture of Ferguson above the Seal of Ohio. These leaflets are paid for with state taxes.

Frank R. Franko, a former Youngstown mayor and municipal judge who was ousted after being charged with fixing tickets, is one of Ferguson's fairground operatives. He is supposed to examine the books of the state highway department. But during the summers, according to his expense reports, he spends a lot of his time driving more than one hundred miles a day back and forth to various fairgrounds.

Campanella has tried to make Ferguson's personal force of fair workers a campaign issue. Campanella, who had one of his campaign workers dig up the pay vouchers and make them available to reporters, charged that Ferguson has wasted $400,000 over two years promoting himself at state expense. Campanella claimed that Ferguson's office has charged time and expenses for attending county fairs to the Ohio Lottery, Ohio Department of Transportation and the Ohio Liquor Department.

"Why did the governor's office approve [the expenditures] if they weren't proper?" Ferguson asked. "If they felt they were wrong, they shouldn't have been approved."

Ferguson should follow the advice found on one of the leaflets he prints:

"Much of the waste and fraud in government can be halted," it reads. "All it takes is your willingness to advise the Auditor of State."

Next time you run into Ferguson or one of his cronies at a county fair, tell him what you think. Be sure to watch out. He may have a crowbar.

August 9, 1982

Wrath of God

The Rev. Ernest Angley, an Akron faith healer, is spouting hellfire. He says he is going to file lawsuits — "and I mean big ones" — against West German authorities who arrested him the other day and charged him with fraud and healing without a license.

The TV evangelist said the police mistreated him. "It was terrible," Angley said. "It was like in Hitler's day. It was like the Gestapo."

To make his point, Angley stripped to a T-shirt at a press conference and displayed bruises on his flabby arms. He railed against the "fascist" German cops.

I'll bet Angley is secretly singing, "Hallelujah!" Any preacher worth a plywood pulpit knows the value of being persecuted. What better way to rouse your flock, gain recognition and new followers, and load donation baskets?

Which could explain the airport rally and the press conferences staged for Angley's return.

Ray Spangler, business manager for Ernest Angley Ministries, acknowledged that the tiff in West Germany last weekend "will help him be much more known in Europe and we're thankful. Many more people will come [to Akron] and see if he has two horns and a tail and then they can make their own decision."

Name a religion and it has its martyrs. If some weren't exactly flayed alive or burned at the stake, their followers were usually able to embellish history a bit.

Hyperbole helps, such as calling your accusers "Hitler" and "Gestapo." Angley even compared his incarceration at a Munich police station with the Passion of Jesus Christ.

"They kept Jesus up all night through, and then they killed

him," the minister said. "They kept me up all night. . . . The testing time came and I wouldn't back down."

Robert I. Abelman and Kimberly A. Neuendorf, professors at Cleveland State University, have just completed a major study of TV evangelists like Angley.

"He couldn't buy that kind of publicity," Abelman said.

The study came up with interesting figures. For example, the average faithful viewer — two hours a day — is asked for more than $138,000 in a year.

"This is direct appeals with a dollar amount," Abelman said, "not just, 'Send us all the money you can.' "

The average cost of a Bible sold by TV evangelists is $192, the study found. Blessed book marks? Don't ask.

Scholars tell us that Christ preached to about 30,000 people; each week, Angley reaches 282,683 households. Whether you think he's a phony or a prophet, it's fascinating television. Angley is even buying the Rev. Rex Humbard's television studio in Akron for $2 million.

Angley tells you he sees demons leaving the bodies of those he heals. He must believe in equal time; he also sees angels standing at his side during his squeal-and-heal services. Not only does God speak to him, Angley sees him, too. Yup, looks just like all those pictures of him.

Angley and God go way back. As a boy of seven, Angley had his first visit from the Almighty. The boy was lying in bed in his family's farmhouse in North Carolina and God showed him millions of stars and told him that was how many souls he would win for Christ.

As far as TV services go, Angley's shows are pretty wild affairs. He gives a sermon, features a few hot numbers from the Grace Cathedral Singing Men and presents videotaped healings from his "Miracle and Salvation" crusades.

If you're too sick to attend a service, Angley has offered this solution: He holds up his hand to the camera and tells you to place your hand on the TV screen. You are now palm to palm with the electronic maestro.

He tells — nay, commands! — the demons to come out of you. He screams, "Heal, Heal! HEEEAALLLL!"

And you wonder why the Germans locked him up.

"They didn't know who I was to begin with," Angley explained, his nasal twang rising and falling with indignation. "They thought I was a small operator. They called America to find out who I was. They didn't know I was big in America. Then they found out I was big and they were in a pickle."

Angley said he was shocked by the foul condition of his jail cell. No windows, a thin mattress, no water and an open, smelly cracked commode.

"Oh, God, please don't let my bowels move while I'm in here," Angley said he prayed. Lucky for him, his prayers were answered.

"Did you hear what happened after I left?" Angley asked. The prime-time preacher read from yesterday's newspaper: hailstones as big as tennis balls pounded West Germany, injuring three hundred people. A woman was killed. Cars crashed. Windows were shattered. The Munich fire department put the damage at tens of millions of dollars.

That's what those Germans get for messing with him, Angley said. God unleashed his wrath.

"God let me know that he would bring judgment," Angley said. "It was like in Moses' day. That's what the Lord told me. He done it again.

"I imagine there's a lot of praying going on in Munich," Angley continued. "Don't you know they're praying. Wouldn't you pray?"

Sure. And can you imagine what God would have done to Munich if they had arrested somebody really big, like Billy Graham?

July 18, 1984

Master Masten

George Forbes' ballyhooed grip on City Council is a wimpy handshake compared to Linndale Mayor Armand Masten's iron-handed domination of this tiny village of 127.

Masten, who has run the village for seventeen years, resembles the clichéd figure from the Old West who was at once mayor, judge, sheriff, undertaker and owner of the town saloon.

Masten is not a mortician — he would probably try it if the state didn't require a license — but he is mayor, judge of Linndale's traffic court, acting police chief and proprietor of Armand's Party Center, 4025 W. 119th Street. Armand's is the site of a famous Prohibition speakeasy and gambling joint, and today it is Linndale's only bar. It serves Italian food and the cook is, yes, Mrs. Masten.

Some Linndale residents say Masten started out with good intentions years ago, but today is a tyrant. He bellows and bullies at meetings. He insists on absolute control of every detail of government. He has hired and fired three police chiefs in six months because they would not do his precise bidding. And he refuses to show public records to reporters asking to see them.

"I run a tight ship," said Masten, a gruff-talking guy with gray hair, aviator glasses and a big western belt buckle.

Most people know Linndale by its police force, one full-time and five part-time. Linndale has the good fortune of being bisected by Interstate 71. This 1,000-foot stretch of freeway is the county's most notorious speed trap and a money-making machine for Linndale.

Last year, the mayor's court reported $117,626 in fines and court costs, which is about 75 percent of the city budget.

Masten may have taken in more, but so far he has refused to let reporters examine his court docket to count the offenses and compare the figures with income. "I don't know what I've got to hide," he said. "If you're looking for something specific, let me know."

The state auditor discovered that the mayor's court was $8,888 short for a six-month period about two years ago. Masten legally is responsible for the mayor's court money, but he blames the former court clerk, Bernice Pyle, for the loss.

"There has been thievery in that town hall since time began," Pyle has countered.

Yesterday, Masten said: "It's time for me to fight back, my friend. They're not going to put me in cahoots with anybody. I'm too much of a bastard to do that."

Meanwhile, Masten and a minority of Linndale Village Council keep duking it out.

At a meeting two days ago, Councilman Vera Vetovitz asked the mayor about the legality of being mayor, judge and police chief simultaneously. He ruled her out of order.

"You're a dictator," she retorted.

The mayor's councilman son, Richard, whom the mayor appointed to a council vacancy, rose to his father's defense. "What good do you do for the community?" Masten the younger demanded. Then he told the 64-year-old woman, "You don't do s---."

This is the same polite fellow who is asking voters in the Ninth District to send him to the Ohio House.

Vetovitz recalled the time years ago when Masten lost his temper, reached across a table at a council meeting, grabbed a council member's nose and attempted to twist it off.

One former Linndale police chief, Edwin C. Donovan, a Cleveland policeman for twenty-five years, lasted three months last summer as the village's chief law officer. "It was like Barney Miller over there, all helter skelter," Donovan said yesterday. "They had no booking procedures as required by state law."

Donovan said confiscated guns and drugs were not kept under control. He said evidence and confiscated property were not logged in books, a standard police procedure.

As a result, a good lawyer would have a field day defending a client charged with a crime in Linndale because police procedures are so sloppy, Donovan said.

And here is a consolation to Cleveland speeders. Donovan said Linndale policemen do not use radar in the properly legal manner.

"All you have to do is plead not guilty if you get a speeding ticket," Donovan said. "Then it goes automatically to Parma [Municipal] Court. Nine out of ten are thrown out. Most of them are bad arrests. Most of them never get that far because once they're transfered out of the mayor's court, [Linndale] loses all the money. So they work out a deal if they can."

Masten was told of Donovan's remarks.

"I don't know what the hell he's talking about," Masten said angrily. "We're not running the Cleveland Police Department here. He's wrong. Mr. Donovan doesn't know a thing about radar. He knows nothing about police work in the community."

Police work in Linndale, when it's not writing speeding tickets, means patroling forty-three acres, keeping children from playing on tree lawns and enforcing the curfew.

Adolph Schultz, Donovan's successor to the $13,700-a-year job, lasted about thirty days last fall. Schultz had one extra duty.

Mayor Masten told the chief he had to eat lunch every day across the street from the police station at, you guessed it, Armand's Party Center.

June 3, 1982

Upholding tradition

News that the mayor of Linndale was charged with two counts of bribery has many Cleveland-area motorists howling with glee.

"Couldn't have happened to a nicer guy," cackled one fellow who's run across Linndale's notorious speed trap on Interstate 71.

Armand Masten, sixty-one, was stung by an FBI-Cleveland Police undercover operation into illegal gambling. Officials have charged Masten with allowing gambling machines in his restaurant, Armand's Place, in exchange for bribes and a piece of the action.

"I don't know anything about gambling," Masten said the other day after he was booked and was slipping out of the Justice Center past TV cameras. "I'm not into gambling, never did, never will. No dice, no horses, nothing."

Since 1965, Masten has ruled Linndale with an iron fist. It's like being king of the sandbox in kindergarten. Linndale, population 127, is about six square blocks.

For a while, Masten not only served as mayor but as police chief, judge of village court and the town's only saloonkeeper.

These responsibilities must have weighed heavily. Not long ago, Masten hired a police chief and closed Armand's Place. He and his son now sell telephones from the site.

People might cheer Masten's apparent downfall, but I won't. First, he hasn't had his day in court. And even if he's found guilty, so what? How can you blame a mayor for carrying on a cherished village tradition?

When Las Vegas was sand and lizards, Linndale was a thriving gambling center of Cleveland.

Linndale's robust practice of wenching, boozing and gambling started before Mayor Harry Dorsey, who served in the 1920s. But Dorsey refined the practice.

During Prohibition, Linndale was rife with speakeasies, gambling dens and fireworks shacks. More than fifty trains stopped there each day as passengers switched from smoke-belching steam engines to electric locomotives allowed to enter Cleveland's modern Union Terminal.

With its roundhouse, coal deck, repair yard and rooming houses, Linndale was a rowdy mix of gandy dancers, signal gangs, wrecking gangs and construction workers.

Dorsey had the misfortune to be caught taking part in the hijacking of a truck stacked with boxes of bootlegged Canadian whiskey. "He spent six months in Leavenworth," said Angelo Mancini, sixty-seven, an amateur historian whose family ran a Linndale grocery store.

Masten may have shanghaied thousands of motorists with his radar-happy police force, but at least he's never been accused of hijacking crates of hooch.

Some councilmen have ripped Masten, calling him a hothead and a dictator. One told of a meeting at which Masten, peeved about something, reached over and tried to twist the nose off the face of an unhappy council member.

Big deal. What's a little nose tweak compared with the antics of Battling Tom O'Malia, Linndale mayor from 1928 to 1932. O'Malia punched hundreds of noses as part of his job.

"A car speeding, a man beating his wife, anything like that, instead of prosecuting them, he'd beat the hell out of 'em," Mancini said. "He'd park his roadster and take care of it with his fists."

O'Malia once remarked: "I can hit hard and shoot straight. I like a good fight, but am strong for nice, clean, peaceful living."

O'Malia didn't disturb Linndale's fine tradition. A decade later, the village justice of the peace, Ethel Sotos, complained: "I'm going to ask the sheriff to clean up this town good. There are all kinds of slot machines and gambling out here. I've asked the marshal a thousand times to clean up."

Other critics have charged Masten with being rude and arrogant. Compared with what?

Some might consider Masten a gentleman compared with Carmen Marano, mayor in 1951 and the former marshal. Marano was once charged with using a blackjack on the head of a woman bar owner.

"I never hit a woman," Marano said at the time. "I hit her husband, though, when he pulled a gun on me." The charges were later dismissed.

Another mayor, John Zelis (1938-1951) knew not to disturb the Linndale way of life. Asked after his election about slot machines, Zelis said: "I'm not going to stop 'em. I expect to be too busy with really important problems, such as unemployment relief for 40 percent of our citizens."

In other communities, mayors get honors for preserving town history. If Masten truly allowed gambling in Linndale, as officials charge, he should be given an appropriate award.

The only problem, I don't think he'd appreciate what the county prosecutor has in mind.

March 8, 1984

Head for the hills

Worried about nuclear war? Has President Reagan's saber rattling got you down?

Relax. Take a few deep breaths. Richard Noble says he's going to save us.

Noble is director of Cuyahoga County Disaster Services. Usually he deals with tornadoes and chemical spills, but he also has an emergency plan for the biggest disaster of all, all-out nuclear war.

In a nutshell, Noble's plan has Cuyahoga County residents fanning out to six rural counties about fifty to sixty miles away.

Wayne County, for example, will get what Noble calls our essential workers — county commissioners, judges, doctors, elected officials and other big shots.

Edward Schuch, fire chief of Wooster, the Wayne County seat, said he's ready for the essential workers.

"We'll have a big tollgate stuck up at the perimeter of the city," he said yesterday. "This is the chance of a lifetime for us to make money. 'Course, we might not get to spend it."

Schuch is struck by the absurdity of preparing for a nuclear holocaust. So is Cuyahoga County Commissioner Ed Feighan.

"Noble told me that in event of a nuclear attack, I'd be spirited off to Wayne County with the other commissioners to carry on the functions of county government," Feighan said yesterday. "I told him, 'If we have a nuclear attack, I'm out of a job. I appreciate your concern, but I don't want to go to Wayne County.' "

Cuyahoga County residents pay Noble $20,230 for his services. Yet he's a guy who got stuck in his Parma driveway during the freak snowstorm two weeks ago and couldn't make it to work. And this is the guy who is supposed to make sure Cuyahoga County's 1.5 million residents make it safely out to the boondocks before the bombs drop?

The premise behind the evacuation plan is that we'll have five days' notice from the Soviets before they blast us.

"The theory behind this is Russia won't start a war without evacuating its people," Noble said. This is supposed to take five days.

Noble has drawn up escape routes for different sectors of Cuyahoga County. For example, Brooklyn, Brook Park, Fairview Park, North Olmsted, Parma, Parma Heights and Linndale residents must escape to Ashland County.

According to the plan, these residents will get into their cars in an orderly fashion, get on Interstate 71 and cruise at 55 miles per hour to Ashland County.

"To facilitate and balance out the traffic movement, those persons driving automobiles with license plates issued during the period of January through June will be advised to leave during the first twelve hours," the plan states. "Those with license plates issued during the period of July through December will be advised to leave during the second twelve hours. Fueling at service stations will be controlled in the same manner."

It's hard to take this stuff seriously. Look what one stalled car on I-71 does during rush hour. And who's going to be working in the filling stations?

Ashland County may be in for a surprise if and when the panicked hordes arrive.

"I just heard about all this," Ashland County Commissioner C. Jay W. Selsh said yesterday. "I know for a fact our disaster services director didn't know that. . . . [Noble] drew up those plans without telling us.

"It's just unbelievable all the pushing and shoving that will go on. It won't work. They'd be killing each other to get out."

Welsh said Ashland was too small to accept all the people who live in those west suburbs and too poor to spend money to provide shelter and shovels and food.

"It's really unthinkable," he said. "I like people in Cleveland, but we're not going to spend money on it. This is a conservative county."

Maybe our federal taxes will be used. President Reagan has asked for $4.2 billion to permit the Federal Emergency Management Agency to get us ready for nuclear war.

Already critics like Sen. Alan Cranston, the California Democrat, have called the idea "faulty and perilous" and a "cruel and dangerous hoax on the American people."

Several communities, including Cambridge, Massachusetts, Boulder, Colorado, and Sacramento County, California, have refused to take part in any evacuation plans.

If the United States evacuates its cities, the Soviets can simply target the evacuation areas, say some Pentagon strategists. The $4.2 billion the President wants to spend for shovels and canned goods and planning will be yet another waste of taxes.

Maybe Noble realizes this, but he can't admit it. His job is to prepare us for the unthinkable.

"Once the bombs go," he said, "it's all over."

April 22, 1982

How juvenile

As you might expect, Cuyahoga County Juvenile Court isn't always a peaceful place.

In its halls and courtrooms on E. 22nd Street, you can find name calling or a shoving match or someone tearing down notices from the bulletin boards.

The childish acts aren't always the work of juvenile delinquents. Sometimes judges are the guilty parties.

There's little love lost between Judge Betty Willis Ruben and Judge John J. Toner. Ruben, three years on the bench, wants to change the county's juvenile justice system. Toner, a 23-year veteran, wants to keep the status quo.

These two are sniping at each other again.

"It's not a personality quarrel," Ruben explained yesterday, "It's a professional quarrel."

Said Toner: "I tried to get along with everybody, but every time I turn around I get stabbed."

The two seemed to clash from Ruben's first month on the bench. Ruben, elected on a reform campaign, began to change some procedures. Toner, the long-time administrative judge, didn't like it.

For example, Ruben posted news clippings about the dangers of drugs and alcohol on bulletin boards in her waiting room.

One day she left town and Toner had the clippings torn down, citing court policy.

Ruben is no shrinking violet. In a memo to Toner, she called the trashing of her bulletin board "the work of a mentally retarded or emotionally disturbed person or even more likely an alcoholic or drug addict."

Hah, take that, you rat.

Toner replied in a memo that her description of the culprit "more properly described the person who posted the material."

Nyah, nyah.

Ruben shot back in a memo: "I am absolutely shocked that you would confess to having come into [my] waiting room . . . [and] deliberately vandalized my bulletin boards . . . . What a great example you set for the children of the community!"

Months later, Ruben's bailiff and Toner got into a shoving match at a copying machine.

The bailiff, Michael Telep, had interested a television news team in investigating the Detention Home. Telep gave them a tour. This angered Toner, who said the bailiff was invading the privacy of the minors.

Later, Telep said Toner confronted him near the copier, grabbing his wrist and shoving him away from the machine. "He [Toner] was wild," Telep, twenty-nine, a former professional football player, said at the time.

To which Toner, sixty-seven, retorted sarcastically: "I hope I didn't hurt him. He's 6-feet-6 inches, I'm 5-feet-11."

Yesterday, Toner remarked: "I might have shaken him upstairs by my vicious attack on him."

The latest Ruben-Toner exchange took place recently. Ruben won't comment on the record about the tiff, but inter-office memos lay it out.

"Yesterday a child came into my courtroom for a hearing from the Detention Home and pleaded that I do something to prevent his getting sexually assaulted when he takes a shower," Ruben wrote in an October 18 memo circulated to the other juvenile judges.

"In January 1984, I will begin my fourth year on the Court. How many more years should I expect to wait before we solve this problem? Why can we not have a child-care worker supervising in the shower room?"

In a snide memo dated the next day and circulated to the judges, Toner responded to Ruben's memo by suggesting that a committee be appointed to study the problem of sex abuse. The committee could be composed of Telep and other Ruben allies, Toner said.

"Without question, all of the above are qualified to produce position papers that are quite repetitive in content," Toner's memo said.

"It was facetious, of course," Toner said yesterday. He added that he truly is concerned about sex abuse at the home.

"[Administrative Juvenile Court] Judge Corrigan had an investigation," Toner said. "There was no sex attack."

So, liar, liar, pants on fire.

No wonder they call it *Juvenile* Court.

November 3, 1983

License to pocket

"Politics is the art of putting people under obligation to you."
— Jacob Arvey, Chicago political boss

If you live around here, you can count on three annoyances: death, taxes and standing in line once a year to get your auto license tags.

The scene yesterday at the privately owned Ohio License Bureau on W. 6th Street was typical: fifteen people on their lunch hours were standing in line, trying to get back to work before their bosses had an excuse to gripe. And this is supposed to be the slow part of the month.

You don't wait in lines for license tags in states like Pennsylvania. You mail a check to Harrisburg and get the tags by return mail.

It sounds like a great idea for Ohio. But greedy politicians won't let us do it.

What most people waiting in license lines yesterday didn't realize was that each was shelling out a $1.50 processing fee that, in large part, ends up in the pockets of political hacks.

The way Ohio validates license plates could have been created by Boss Tweed. It's a political spoils system based on party patronage. Here's how it works:

A governor is elected. In each county, he appoints a party loyalist, usually the party chairman, to run the profitable monopoly business of dishing out license tags.

When Jim Rhodes was governor, this juicy political plum in Cuyahoga County went to Bob Bennett, the Republican party bigwig and businessman. By the end of his eight-year reign as License Boss, after paying rents and salaries, Bennett reportedly was earning net profits of about $70,000 a year.

Not bad for a part-time job.

When Dick Celeste took the helm, he made Brooklyn Mayor John Coyne the county License Boss. Coyne took over Bennett's business — the various office leases, the office equipment, the bookkeeping system, everything but the Republicans who held the top twenty-five salaried jobs. Coyne dumped them and installed his Democratic friends — just as Bennett had fired the Democrats when he took over.

Coyne cut some salaries and expenses and may net up to $150,000 a year with the monopoly Celeste granted him. Hardly chump change.

"I hope it's true," Coyne said yesterday. "Then we wouldn't have so many people running for Congress and governor. This has got to be the best job in the world."

Coyne said he wouldn't keep all his profits. "I expect to get a reasonable wage to compensate for my time," he explained. "The rest will go for candidates."

"C'mere," he went on, moving to another room at party headquarters. "See this computer. $11,000. Bought for the Democratic Party from the [license] proceeds."

The party's 1983 annual report, however, didn't reflect any contributions from Coyne.

Suppose you don't like the idea of your license fee ending up on a politician's Form 1040. Tough. You don't have a choice. You can't vote against a License Boss. You can't even find out what he does with your money.

Over the years, a few foolhardy state legislators have tried to remove patronage from the license system. State Auditor Thomas Ferguson gave it a shot several years ago. Some Republicans even made noise about reform.

State legislators of both parties looked at these reform-minded colleagues like they were lunatics: "You're kidding. No booty for the victors? What have you been smoking lately?"

"It's an outrage and should be abolished," Tim Hagan, the Democratic county commissioner, said of the license patronage. "I'm on the side of the angels on this one.

"No one should make the excessive profits that Bennett or anyone else made at the expense of the public. The public has no choice. It's a monopoly. It was wrong under Rhodes and it's wrong under Celeste."

It's no surprise that Bennett, the one-time beneficiary, defends the system as he does.

"I think it's a phony baloney issue," he said. "I defy anybody to tell me [state] bureaucrats can do it cheaper. . . . All Tim [Hagan] wants to do is increase the costs. I support John Coyne on this."

Back at the license bureau on W. 6th Street, May Allen was waiting in line.

"What can you do about it?" she asked. She laughed wearily. "I'd like to get some of the money myself."

Behind her, a bearded guy, Harry Andrist, said: "I can't understand why people tolerated the system for so long. It's an outrage. It's a holdover from a different era.

"It's a waste of time to stand in line, too," Andrist, a chemistry prof at Cleveland State University, went on.

"Why can't the tags come in the mail like the boat tags from the Department of Natural Resources?"

January 26, 1984

Salesman Forbes

You live in Cleveland. You are being asked by your political leaders to let them raise your income taxes. So what do you do?

If you care about your city — most people do — you think about the request and then vote with good intentions.

Cleveland voters aren't cheapskates. When the city defaulted, voters knew it needed help. In February 1979, they increased their city income taxes by half, from 1 percent to 1.5 percent.

In 1981, the recession was crushing the local economy. Voters knew it and shelled out. They pushed the income tax to 2 percent, doubling city taxes in two years.

Our leaders are making a sales pitch again: raise the income tax to 2.5 percent because we will be running a $17 million deficit.

So far, their sales job stinks.

To be convinced to buy something, you require a measure of two things from the salesman — respect and trust.

A salesman has to be respectful. If a salesman acts like an arrogant jerk, you walk out of the store, telling yourself, "I wouldn't buy nickels for four cents from the guy."

And you have to trust what the salesman says. If he misleads you — says it's fresh bread when it's really two days old — you'd eat rice before going back to his bakery.

City Council President George L. Forbes could use a course in salesmanship. He's sabotaging the tax hike by being an arrogant jerk.

Forbes is asking voters to give him more tax dollars to administer. At the same time, when asked by a TV reporter about a past-due water bill, Forbes responded like a moron.

For those of you who missed Carl Monday's recent interview with Forbes on WJKW Channel 8, the following is being reprinted as a public service.

Monday showed Forbes a record of the public servant's past-due water bill.

Forbes: "No big problem. The city ain't gonna go bankrupt."

Monday: "Don't you think it's a bad example to set?"

"No, I do not. I don't have the money."

"You don't have the money to pay a $400 water bill?"

"I do not have the money."

Forbes went into the meeting room, then, after a few seconds, came back through the glass door.

"I gave you a (bleeping) answer," the elected official said.

"And I gave you a follow-up question," the reporter replied.

"I gave you a (bleeping) answer. One of these days I'm gonna kick your (behind)! It might be this (bleeping) one! You got your (bleeping) answer, now get out of my face!"

Reporter: "Thank you. OK."

"I ain't bull(bleeping) you! I'll take that (bleeping) camera and wrap it around your (bleeping) head! One of these days, you're gonna grab me at the wrong (bleeping) minute! OK? I ain't bull(bleeping) with you!"

"We got a meeting," Councilman Lonnie Burten told Forbes, trying to break it up.

The Council President carried on: "I'll kick your (bleeping) (behind)! Son of a (bleep)."

You would think that a guy who has a law firm, several big real estate ventures and a wife with radio stations could pay a $400 water bill on time.

Yesterday, Forbes said he still hadn't paid the bill and wouldn't discuss the incident. Nor would he talk about the merits of his hard-sell philosophy on a city tax increase.

If Forbes truly wants to sell us a tax hike, he could try something like this:

"Look, we're going to trim any fat from the budget. There isn't much. We're also going to try to collect every penny owed us by deadbeats. We'll beg workers near sixty-five or older to retire.

"Meanwhile, we're going to have to cut city services. We'll try to cut those you need least. If we can't make it, we'll come back to you and ask you to raise taxes."

Instead, Forbes used a club. If people won't raise taxes, he said, "we'll close down their health centers. We'll close down the fire stations."

That's blackmail. Voters know it and don't like it.

If he wants to sell voters on a tax hike, Forbes will need a new sales pitch.

Otherwise, voters might respond in a way he understands:

"Take that ballot box and shove it up your (bleep)."

February 27, 1984

Smut analysis

No doubt you've read stories about federal grants being squandered on wacky studies.

Dr. Judith Reisman, who received a Ph.D. from Case Western Reserve University for a 1980 thesis explaining why Dorothy Fuldheim gets so much mail, has snagged such a grant. She was given $800,000 to analyze cartoons in *Playboy* and *Penthouse*. Her thesis is that this smut may be linked to juvenile crime.

Pornography and crime are certainly worthy of scientific study. But with her credentials and methods, Reisman may be setting some kind of record for government waste.

Some of you may doubt she can set a record. After all, she faces tough competition:

There was the $6,000 grant to study how pot smoking affects scuba divers. Conclusion: reefers and reefs don't mix.

Remember the $45,000 dished out to determine how long it takes to make breakfast? You'll be glad to know it takes 0.5 seconds to crack an egg.

The FAA even spent $57,900 to study the body measurements of one airline's stewardess trainees. Purely for safety reasons, of course.

I think Reisman, a former Clevelander, and her $800,000 grant may just top all of these. This view is supported by some research psychologists.

For example, University of California psychologist Gilbert Geis, the grant reviewer for the Center for Crime and Delinquency, read her proposal. He was quoted as saying:

"I've never seen anything like this in thirty-three years. It's just a crazy, wild proposal. She doesn't know anything about statistics. . . . I wouldn't fund this grant in a million years. I don't know anyone who would fund this grant."

He underestimates the Office of Juvenile Justice and Delinquency Prevention, part of the Justice Department. The office and its director, Alfred S. Regnery, a Reagan appointee and former official with Young Americans for Freedom, gave the $800,000 to Reisman — without competition, peer review, or announcing the money was available.

Regnery has been criticized for using his ideology in deciding how to grant his $15 million in research funds.

Reisman, who said she wrote such songs as "Mary Magic Morning" and "A Proper Breakfast" for the *Captain Kangaroo* show, has come under congressional fire for her controversial porno grant. Sen. Howard Metzenbaum, Democrat of Ohio, and others on the Juvenile Justice Subcommittee of the Senate Judiciary Committee asked her on August 1 how she got a Ph.D. without finishing college.

She told them CWRU gave her credit for "life experience" and let her into speech communications graduate school. Reisman also listed on her resumé a non-existent professorship at Haifa University.

Her dissertation, "A Rhetorical Analysis of Dorothy Fuldheim's Television Commentaries," looked at twelve Fuldheim editorials. About 180 pages later, Reisman concluded: "Her heartfelt sympathy is the secret of Fuldheim's success. She is what she aspires to be for all of us. She is an honest, a caring human being — a good woman, skilled in speaking."

For this, a doctorate from a respected university?

Reisman has little background in research or psychology, but it apparently doesn't matter. She makes up for it with originality.

For instance, she told a Washington, D.C., radio audience that Alfred Kinsey, the respected, pioneering scientist, "was involved in what amounted to the vicious genital torture of hundreds of children."

She also stated that Kinsey "had sex with animals" and "had absolutely no objection at all to male use of children sexually."

Officials at the Kinsey Institute at Indiana University dismiss her notions as nonsense.

Her radio host, conservative Patrick Buchanan, asked her why this information had not emerged in the thirty years since Kinsey published his groundbreaking studies on human sexuality.

"It is a gigantic scandal," she responded. "It is so shocking I suspect that professionals who read the information simply could not encompass the idea."

Regnery was alerted to Reisman's radio performance, and she was invited to the Office of Juvenile Justice and Delinquency Prevention. Within two weeks, a stunningly short time to write a proposal and get a grant, Reisman was awarded the $800,000 for her two-year study.

You may wonder what Reisman, who was paid $44,000 a year from the grant, has to say about all this. You're in for a long wait. She said through her secretary that she was too busy to come to the phone and explain what she's doing with the taxpayers' money.

But she did give the senators a peek at her work in progress at the recent hearing. From her briefcase, she pulled out fifty or sixty bound pages and said she knew the senators would want to see this.

No text, just pages and pages of smutty cartoons clipped and pasted from *Playboy, Penthouse,* and *Hustler.*

"No question," said Roy Myers, press aide to Metzenbaum. "It appears she was saying, 'This is my work.' "

In that case, what's the fuss about credentials? She doesn't need a doctorate to cut and paste. Kindergarten is plenty.

August 10, 1984

View from the top

A headline in a Columbus newspaper caught my eye: "Hicks up north can take a back seat to Columbus."

It was a column about how Columbus has passed Cleveland as the state's most populous city. The writer went on to call Cleveland "Rubesville," and its citizens "a bunch of small-town hicks."

Across the country, small-town hicks journey to the Big City to check out the action. Since Clevelanders are now supposed to be hicks, I decided to make a visit to No. 1 city.

I zipped by the Columbus city limit sign. About half a tank of gas later, I hit downtown. Meanwhile, for miles and miles, I drove past cornfields and vacant land. That explained all those Columbus TV commercials for corn fertilizer.

Downtown, while looking for a place to eat lunch, I noticed that the pedestrians stood frozen on the curbs while waiting for traffic lights to change. They wouldn't even take a half step off the curb on the yellow.

It's been said that teeming big cities can turn people into robots, but this was amazing.

Until someone explained it to me: Columbus police are tough on crime. They ruthlessly ticket jaywalkers. They once even busted a little old lady who was sweeping the curb in front of her home.

Later, I stopped with two colleagues for a drink. One ordered white wine.

The bartender brought the wine to our table and plunked it down. It was *Inglenook* in what resembled a tiny salad dressing bottle with a metal screw cap. The reporter twisted off the cap and poured the wine into a glass.

Now that's big-city sophistication, I thought.

Seeking night life, I checked a glossy $2.95 Columbus guide sold on newsstands. The first sentence under the heading "Night Life" held promise:

"Let's not kid ourselves. Columbus doesn't have a reputation for being the most swingingest town around."

For a No. 1 city, these experiences seemed odd. I did some research.

For years, Columbus has been on a feeding frenzy. The city reminds you of one of those creatures from a B-grade science fiction movie. The Blob That Ate Central Ohio.

Columbus has been annexing outlying cornfields, vacant land, kiddie sandboxes — any stretch of earth it can swallow. From 1950 to 1980, the Blob was busy. It almost quintupled in size from thirty-nine to 181 square miles.

Now the Blob wants respect as No. 1.

Pat Baker, an officer in the Columbus Area Chamber of Commerce, explained how people feel about being the No. 1 city.

"The response we hear is, 'It's about time,' " Baker said. "People are proud. They're excited."

What do people outside the state think of Columbus?

Baker had the answer. The Chamber of Commerce had completed a study. Results?

"There hasn't been any conclusive research that shows that Columbus is known for anything," Baker said.

Exactly.

Actually, Columbus is the birthplace of the two-way QUBE television. And a marketing prof at Ohio State University came up with a claim the city can make — "the interactive television capital of the world."

That has a nice ring to it. But what sensible city would really want to brag to the world that its citizens interact with TVs all the time? Inner City Corn Capital of the World would be a lot classier.

In comparison, Cleveland is the birthplace of the electric streetcar, the first street lights, the first U.S. diesel engine, the first modern golf ball, and the list goes on.

Besides QUBE television, Columbus can boast of being . . . well, the birthplace of the Wendyburger.

So how did Columbus get to be No. 1 with these shortcomings?

It's no big secret that the people of Columbus had nothing to do with building their city. Ohio taxpayers, you and I, built the Blob That Ate Central Ohio.

The largest employer in Columbus is state government with 20,000 workers. The No. 2 employer is Ohio State University with 16,500, again, built by taxes. The No. 3 employer is the federal government. The fourth and fifth largest employers are the Columbus school systems and the city government. You get the idea.

Columbus isn't a city at all. It's a bureaucracy.

April 19, 1984

5
RIGHTS & WRONGS

IRS bites back

The IRS thinks Anne McNally of Lakewood is a menace to our tax system.

McNally has not thrown tea bales into a harbor. She has not urged us to withhold the taxes that build bombs. She has not joined forces with Posse Comitatus, the militant tax protesters.

McNally's dangerous act: she scribbled critical remarks about the government on her federal income tax returns.

For this, the Internal Revenue Service decided to teach this ex-school teacher a lesson, even though she fills out her returns correctly and pays what she owes.

Citing a 1982 law, the IRS fined McNally $500 for filing what it called a "frivolous" tax return.

When April 15 rolls around, most people get the urge to bellow, moan, rant, rave, weep or gnash their teeth. McNally is different because she expresses her frustrations on her Form 1040. Why does she do it?

"Maybe it is the only contact I have with government," she explained. "This is the agency that is very involved in all our lives."

McNally, an office manager, became an IRS pen pal around the time of Watergate.

"I really have not been writing vile things," said McNally, a pleasant woman with short gray hair and glasses. "I write notes about the government, the politicians." For instance, McNally wrote on her 1972 return: "It seems like Russia when it comes to taxes. You get more from a paycheck than I do."

Another year, at the bottom of her return, above her signature, she crossed out the words that said she swore everything she had filled out was true. Instead she wrote in: "I think you should get a few politicians in Washington to swear to be honest."

One year, she jabbed at President Richard M. Nixon. Another year she wrote some verse about Washington architecture, saying it looked like it had been designed by Albert Speer, Hitler's notorious armaments boss.

McNally, a graduate of Notre Dame Academy and Western Reserve University, likes to read. Sometimes she included magazine articles about taxes in her return.

On her 1983 return, McNally said she bet that she paid more taxes than ex-presidents and the wealthy. On the envelope across the IRS address, she wrote, "Fund for ex-actors, illegal armaments for dictators."

All in all, pretty tame stuff.

The IRS fine rattled her.

"I was shocked and I was paranoid and angry," McNally said. "I got a copy of the Constitution out and I re-read the Bill of Rights. I didn't know what to think."

The IRS didn't tell McNally whether her 1982 or 1983 return was judged to be frivolous. (The others don't fall under the new law.) Nor did she get a hearing.

"They can't do this," she decided. "To arbitrarily say, 'Here's a person we're going to fine. This person has no voice in the matter. This person cannot make an appeal until the fine has been paid. Cannot meet a judge. Cannot meet any individual involved in this process.' "

McNally decided to act.

"I made up my mind I was going to see it through," she said. "I wrote to the ACLU [American Civil Liberties Union] initially. I sat down and I had to make a decision on whether I would do this. Whether it would affect my life, my job or my future.

"No matter what, I [decided] I was going to pursue this because I thought this was an important issue. And I felt I should not back down. I felt I'd be a coward if I did not stand up and tell them, 'No, you can't do this.'

"If I turned my back on the situation, I'd be turning my back on my beliefs and my country."

The Cleveland ACLU office plans to appeal the IRS ruling by pointing out to the IRS there's such a thing as the First Amendment, that McNally can write anything she pleases on her tax return. The ACLU will also argue that McNally was denied due process.

So far, the IRS has socked 5,528 tax-payers with $500 fines for supposedly filing frivolous returns.

Rod Young, an IRS spokesman in Washington, was asked about the logic of fining people who scribble nasty notes on tax returns.

In a few cases, he said, the IRS "may have applied penalties when they shouldn't have." He wouldn't discuss McNally's case.

McNally hopes she wins her tax appeal, but she isn't bitter.

"I thank God that I was born in this country," she said. "The way I have spoken out many times in my life, I wouldn't have lasted so long in other countries."

June 7, 1984

A matter of record

He made a mistake twenty-three years ago and has been paying for it since.

Jim Berg was tending bar one afternoon at the Lark-Ridge Tavern in Lakewood. A regular was drinking at the bar.

"I didn't like the guy to start with," Berg said. "His wife called the bar and complained that she didn't have any money for groceries, that he was spending it all drinking."

Berg, a 1951 grad of Cathedral Latin High School, was twenty-eight years old at the time. He should have known better than to shove his face in a marital spat. He told the lush to cut the boozing and give his wife money to buy food.

"This guy didn't want to listen," Berg recalled. "One word led to another. There was an unloaded .38 with no firing pin under the bar. I used it to scare this guy out. It was a mistake."

Berg got nervous. He put the gun in his pocket and left the bar for his car. Lakewood police, always quick answering complaints, arrived and arrested Berg. He was charged with carrying a concealed weapon, a felony.

Berg was found guilty and sentenced to three years in prison, an almost unheard of sentence for a first offender today. Berg served two years.

"I paid for the crime," he said. "I paid for it the hard way. In this day and age, they probably wouldn't bother going to court for a concealed weapon charge."

With his record, Berg didn't have to worry about being flooded with job offers after he got out of jail. He went into business for himself painting houses. He wife died in 1973 and Berg has lived alone since.

Two years ago, he paid a lawyer, Thomas R. McNamara, to seal his criminal record. It was easy. The lawyer told Common Pleas Judge Roy F. McMahon the truth about Berg: that he'd been a very good boy since 1960.

The judge ordered Berg's record sealed. Mentions of Berg's name in court indexes and journals were blacked out.

It was a fair decision. Our society makes people pay for crimes. Once they pay and prove they're clean, then our laws say the former offenders deserve to be treated like everybody else.

Under the law, Berg now is supposed to have all the rights and privileges of any citizen. For example, Berg doesn't have to tell about his sealed record on job applications. And it's a misdemeanor for someone to reveal Berg's sealed record.

But thanks to computerized records, employers and their investigators have little trouble turning up information that should be secret.

Meanwhile, the recession knocked the ladders from under Berg's small painting business. He decided to get a job with pension and health care benefits. A couple of months ago, he applied as a security guard at Huntington Bank.

The bank has an ex-FBI agent who runs security checks. He discovered that a case about Berg had been sealed.

"I told them this is supposed to be expunged," Berg said. "My lawyer called them. I don't know what he said. I got the job."

Berg worked for three weeks. "I was never so happy," he said.

Meanwhile, the bank sent his fingerprints to the BCI, the Ohio Bureau of Criminal Information. His conviction record there apparently had not been sealed. A report came back saying Berg had served time for carrying a concealed weapon.

"I feel bad for the guy," said Jerome Sklarek, head of security. "I like Jim very much. He was a nice man, twenty-some years without a record, but he had to be bonded. He'd be carrying a firearm and he was convicted of CCW. It was a no-win situation."

Replied Berg: "I'm out of a job, I'm mad and I don't think it's right."

Berg's story was told to John Chmielewski, who oversees criminal records in the county clerk's office.

"We get a lot of phone calls like that," he said. "People say, 'Hey, why can't I get a job. My record was sealed.'

"We advise them to go back to their attorney and touch all the bases. We don't like to get into, 'Hey, the attorney blew it.' A lot of attorneys do not know they are supposed to get a copy and serve all these different agencies — FBI, BCI, sheriff."

"We used to send copies to the FBI and everything," Chmielew-ski went on. "We got sued because we didn't send something to some little police department. Then the prosecutor said we don't have to notify anybody, just seal our records."

"I was retained to get an order of expungement and I did," said Berg's lawyer, McNamara. "The same process that gets his record on the computer ought to work the other way to get it off. There's a hole in the system. It's an impossibility to notify every law enforcement agency."

Berg was in no mood for explanations. "I know it was supposed to be taken care of and I got fired," he said. "I'm not going to rest on this. Maybe it will help somebody else out."

He calmed down and added: "If I could get my job back, I'd give my right arm."

October 10, 1983

A modern day Paine

"It will be the docility of modern man that will be our undoing."
— Georges Bernanos, 1942

Our times have been described as a new era of McCarthyism. Literature is banned from library shelves, government surveillance encroaches on civil liberties, Red-baiting is back in fashion.

So civil libertarians, armed with speech and pencils and legal briefs, are out sounding the alarm. At the front lines in the attack on docility and censorship is tireless Nat Hentoff.

It's hard to pigeonhole Hentoff, to describe him in a phrase. He has written books about jazz, education, the First Amendment and government surveillance, not to mention novels and children's books. He delivers speeches about the press, drug addiction and the FBI.

Hentoff reminds you of a modern-day Thomas Paine, a fierce champion of the Bill of Rights. Maybe "patriot" is the word to describe him.

Hentoff visited Cleveland recently to speak about censorship at the annual convention of the Ohio Library Association. He is short, a young-looking fifty-seven, with curly black-and-gray hair and a full beard.

Censorship in public schools is a hot topic these days. The American Library Association has found that the number of book challenges tripled in 1981 to nearly one thousand. Many were prompted by conservative lobby groups like the Moral Majority and Phyllis Schlafly's Eagle Forum.

These groups have found offensive such books as John Steinbeck's *Grapes of Wrath,* J.D. Salinger's *Catcher in the Rye,* William Shakespeare's *The Merchant of Venice* and the *American*

Heritage Dictionary of the English Language.
Some parents are upset that these books contain what they consider offensive words. Other parents consider book banning a waste of time, noting that children hear more vulgar words on the playground and at home than they could find in the banned literature.

"Any time you start to ban words, to punish words, you're in very grave trouble," Hentoff said during a recent interview at a downtown hotel. "That means, eventually, there'll be a list of prohibited words. And it will depend on who is in power to decide which words are too offensive or too dangerous to be used . . . [but] speech is protected, no matter how vile.

"There's more of this since Reagan was elected. Not that he's given speeches saying, 'Go ban books.' But a lot of people feel his election validated their concerns about the family and traditional values and all that stuff. Before that, you had not only right-wingers, as you do now, but you had blacks trying to ban *Huckleberry Finn,* feminists trying to ban elementary textbooks because of sexist stereotypes and so on. . . .

"From the beginning of the new surge [of book banning], I was very impressed with the librarians," Hentoff said. "Librarians used to be stereotyped as softspoken, scared people who didn't want to cause trouble. Actually, they're very courageous. I think they're much more courageous on the First Amendment front than most other people, including journalists, because their jobs are right on the line."

Hentoff perhaps is best known for writing a column, since 1958, in the *Village Voice* and for his work as a *New Yorker* staff writer since 1960. He was an editor at *Downbeat,* the jazz magazine, and, until recently, he wrote a jazz column for *Cosmopolitan.* He lives in Greenwich Village with his wife, Margot.

He describes himself as an advocacy writer.

"I think if you can get people excited — whether they're excited against you or for you — on public issues, that's a very valuable thing to do," he explained. "That's the hardest thing to do: to arouse people. Not because they're not interested in the issues. Most people say, 'What the hell can you do about it.'

"But if a reporter can, through a piece or a series, get them angry, that means they have become citizens again. They're sufficiently involved so they want to know, 'Why the hell don't we do something about this stuff.' That's very valuable. Papers that don't do that are, to me, only good for the comic strips."

In the past year, Hentoff is proudest of his reporting on the FBI's undercover sting operation, Abscam. He said he was the first journalist to write about what he considered civil liberties infringements by the FBI. He noted that the FBI violated its own guidelines in snaring congressmen in Abscam.

"I've been yelling and screaming out there and finally got something done," Hentoff said. "I think eventually we'll get some legislation to circumscribe the FBI. One of the things that makes this [Abscam] stuff so dangerous is you can use it not only in political corruption cases, but also against nuclear activists or anybody you want to entrap.

" . . . Because an agent is undercover, he doesn't need a judicial warrant. He can do whatever he likes for as long as he wants to. It's just crazy. It's a police state.

"I think I was the first one to write about it in any detail. I went through the due-process motion hearings. The rest of the press just fell for it. They got their leaks. And they thought this was just fine — you got corrupt politicians, what could be better."

Despite people's worries about today being a new era of McCarthyism, Hentoff said our civil liberties were under far greater attack seven years after the Founding Fathers wrote the Bill of Rights.

In 1798, Congress was dominated by the Federalists, an elitist group which considered government the province of the upper class. The Federalists passed the Alien and Sedition Acts, and in the next two years, four newspaper editors were fined and imprisoned for criticizing the U.S. government.

But, as Hentoff wrote in his latest book, *The First Freedom: The Tumultuous History of Free Speech in America* (Delacorte, 1980), public outrage over repressive legislation put Thomas Jefferson in the White House in 1801. He pardoned those convicted and Congress repaid the fines.

"Speech is sacred, no matter how awful, because everything else we do — politics, free association — is based on speech," Hentoff said. "That's why no one should punish speech."

November 7, 1982

Slipping through the net

Bernice Johnson never really recovered from her nervous breakdown in 1975.

She could go to the store and buy potatoes and beans and greens. She could cook for herself and clean her two-room East Cleveland apartment. And she could figure out how to catch the bus and keep her appointments with Dr. James E. Fleming.

"[But] she was only marginally functional," said Fleming, a former Case Western Reserve University medical school instructor. "She was just grossly inadequate. Her level of tension was so high."

A few of her problems: hypertension, chronic peptic ulcers, paranoia, residual schizophrenia, chronic anxiety neurosis, borderline intellect.

Johnson was in and out of Huron Road Hospital in 1981, the year she received an unusual letter from the Social Security Administration.

The May 15 letter told her she wasn't disabled anymore and that she was able to hold a job. The letter said the benefits she had been receiving since January 1975 were cut off. The letter noted that she could appeal this decision.

Johnson, forty-eight at the time, was stunned. How would she survive without the $264 in monthly benefits?

She had held a job for five years as a nurse's aide. But that was a decade ago. "Where am I going to live?" she asked Fleming. "How am I going to get money to live on?"

"She was consumed by it," Fleming recalled. "She was upset about it all the time. . . . The stress of that whole ordeal was extremely taxing. She was full of anxiety, irritability, fear. . . . It aggravated her underlying problems."

Johnson's mother, Theresa Kidd, sixty-nine, said: "She was doing fine until they told her she was going to be cut off. Well, what we call fine."

Dr. Fleming was not surprised by Johnson's plight. Increasingly, he has been seeing disabled people purged from the Social Security disability benefit rolls. The Reagan administration, in an effort to cut costs of the $22 billion a year disability insurance system, has knocked 200,000 people from the rolls in the last fiscal year.

Lately, congressional critics have been blasting the Reagan administration, charging it with making cold and capricious cuts. Nearly all the cutoffs are appealed (about a nine-month process), and half are overturned by the appeals board.

But here's the shame. The disabled go without their benefits as they shoulder the burden of proof, getting statements from their doctors to prove their disability. More than a dozen deaths linked to the cutoffs have been documented by the House Select Committee on Aging.

Reagan had promised he wouldn't destroy the so-called safety net, the web of benefits that keep alive the helpless and the truly desperate.

But Johnson's story shows Reagan's promise to be an empty sham.

With help from her relatives, she began her appeal. Since she was sick most of last year, she missed several appointments with the appeals board.

Johnson's mother said her daughter received a letter this year that in effect said: "This is your last chance. Come to a meeting on February 27 or we're throwing out your appeal."

On that day, Johnson got a ride downtown from a friend. The meeting lasted about an hour. She was a nervous wreck. Afterwards, she felt the meeting had gone very badly. She told her mother she knew her benefits were cut off permanently.

Johnson continued to break down. She couldn't breathe. Her family took her to Fleming, who put her in Huron Road Hospital.

Later that day, despite intensive care, Johnson died.

"It was an acute respiratory attack," Fleming said. The doctor said the disability cutoff created "an unusually taxing and stressful situation that aggravated" the problems that in turn caused her death.

Johnson might still be alive today if disability benefits were allowed to continue while an appeal is pending. Sen. Howard Metzenbaum, the Ohio Democrat, and other congressmen are pressuring the Reagan administration to adopt this rule.

On April 22, 1982, a letter arrived for Johnson. It was good news from Social Security.

The letter said in effect: We made a mistake. Your benefits should not have been cut off a year ago. You're getting them all back.

"The enclosed decision is favorable to you," the letter read. "If you are satisfied with the decision, there is no need for you to do anything at the present time."

Bernice Johnson couldn't do anything about the good news. She had been dead for six weeks.

September 23, 1983

The joyride

Like all of us, he has the right to be left alone. Like most of us, he gets mad when jerks abuse that right.

Dan Lehlbach, thirty-two years old, paints a dozen or two houses a year. You've probably never heard of him. His only advertising is a three-foot sign, Sun Painting, in front of his North Olmsted home.

The other day, Lehlbach began getting a series of annoying telephone sales pitches. He recalled one conversation:

An upbeat huckster called and told Lehlbach he could win a free gift worth $500 to $2,500. All Lehlbach had to do was order a thousand pens or a thousand key chains emblazoned with his company logo.

Lehlbach told the salesman to forget it. He didn't have a company logo. He wasn't in the market for key chains.

"Are you crazy?" the salesman asked. "You'd turn down a free gift?"

"I paint about six houses a year," said Lehlbach, trying to make a point. "What am I gonna do, give each customer 150 key chains?"

"You some kind of wise guy?"

"Look, you called me," Lehlbach said. "I don't want any of your — "

The phone intruder interrupted: "You got some kinda problem?"

On it went. Lehlbach, a former bartender, doesn't like being pushed around. So he got the caller's name — Mike Mitchell — and for whom he worked — Cameo Marketing Inc., in Mineola, New York.

The huckster probably hadn't been driving through North Olmsted scouting sales leads. So Lehlbach asked him where he got his number.

Dun & Bradstreet, Mitchell told him.

That explained it. A few weeks earlier, Dun & Bradstreet, the giant business information firm, asked Lehlbach to fill out an application.

"I couldn't figure it out," the house painter said. "I haven't asked for a bank loan or for credit from suppliers."

Dun & Bradstreet told Lehlbach how great it is to be in its computers: it was like having "a super credit card" and he could get loans and new customers and new lines of merchandise. "It can't hurt," he was told.

So Lehlbach filled out the form, listing assets — scaffolding, ladders, painting gear — and other credit information. Dun & Bradstreet neglected to mention it would be putting his name on a list and selling it to sales companies.

Lehlbach told of another typical call: "This other idiot caught me off guard. It was 8 a.m. and I was just getting up. He said I could win a gold chain in a black velvet jewelry box worth $500. All I had to do was buy this ad with him."

After finding out the guy got his name from a Dun & Bradstreet list, Lehlbach told him he wasn't interested.

"I'm offering you a chance at $500 of free gold," the huckster said.

"I don't want it."

"You dumb [bleep]."

Lehlbach called Dun & Bradstreet and asked that his name be left off its lists to phone solicitors. The calls stopped after that.

I called Ray Robbin, general manager of Cameo Marketing, to ask from what school of telephone etiquette his sale force graduated.

This is frustrating work, Robbin said. People aren't exactly clogging his phone banks with orders to snatch up personalized pens and key rings.

"The average businessman is not the brightest person in the world," said Robbin, expounding his philosophy of selling. "He realizes deep down he needs our item to survive. But he doesn't want to buy it."

So his salesmen, who make up to twenty calls an hour to people they think are dumb, occasionally have to blow off steam.

"If someone gives you a hard time, we have what we call a 'joy-ride' with 'em," Robbin said.

A "joyride," he explained, is when a phone huckster gets his jollies by abusing, berating or insulting someone who won't buy a thousand hokey key chains.

"Generally, you do it when somebody was a total wise guy," Robbin said. "Maybe one out of two hundred calls."

Either Dan Lehlbach is a total wise guy or Mike Mitchell has very sensitive feelings.

"Ah, Mr. Mitchell is no longer with us," Robbin said. "He was saying a few wrong things on the phone."

November 14, 1983

Unwanted calls

I'm a quiet type of person," the guy was saying. "I deliver mail. When I come home, I'm dead tired. I really don't have a lot of time to spare."

That sounds normal.

"I'm single," he went on. "I once studied for the priesthood. I read a lot, study a lot. I write. I can't be bothered with phone calls by anybody who gets on my phone."

We know the feeling.

"I'd like to keep my phone calls to people who are close to me," said the guy, Robert Durback, fifty-one, of Fairview Park. "I don't want to be bothered by someone calling me to see if I want to subscribe to *Glamour* magazine. That's why I've got an unlisted phone number."

Durback pays Ohio Bell Telephone Company $18 a year to keep his number confidential.

So that solves your problem with annoying junk phone calls, right?

Wrong. "I keep getting computerized phone calls," Durback said. "One I got, the voice said, 'This is a computer.' I said, 'I don't talk to computers,' and hung up."

About a week ago, Durback said he answered his ringing phone only to hear the cloying voice of a salesman from Ohio Motorists Association, the AAA in this area. "I asked him where he got my phone number," Durback said. "He said, 'Our computer supplies us with our phone listings.' I told him to remove my number from his computer because I have an unlisted phone number."

Way to go, Bob. That must have solved your problem with annoying calls from AAA solicitors.

Wrong. "A week later, I got a call," Durback explained. "It was a young male. He said his name was Chris and he was calling for Triple A. I stopped him right there. I said my number was unlisted and that I wanted to talk to his supervisor. His response was '[Bleep] you!' and he hung up on me."

Well, at least you got him off the phone.

Not exactly. "The phone rang immediately," Durback said. "I answered and there was nothing. I hung up and it rang immediately again. So I fixed him good. I shut my phone off."

But Durback can't keep his phone off forever. And he doesn't think he should have to put up with phone peddlers who put profit above his privacy. "I don't like the idea of companies not respecting my privacy and calling my unlisted number that I'm paying Ohio Bell to protect," Durback said. "I think it's very rude. They're thinking in terms of marketing and profits and that's fine. But this is my home. They have no business barging into my living room, whether it's through my front door or through my telephone."

A call was made to Jerry Turk, spokesman for Ohio Motorists Association, to ask about AAA's phone solicitations.

"We have an ongoing program," he explained. "We try not to call somebody twice."

But you called this guy who has an unlisted number.

"That can happen, I suppose," Turk said. He said that the thirty or forty phone solicitors pick an exchange number — for instance, 333 for Fairview Park — then call every number in sequence.

Well, that explains how you reached Durback. But your solicitor had a rather unusual way to close a sale. He told the customer, "[Bleep] you."

"I never heard that one before," Turk said. "If it ever happened, we regret it very much. I'm not saying it's not possible."

That doesn't do Durback's privacy much good. He thinks our legislators should pass a law requiring companies to call only people with listed phone numbers, or better yet, only people who have an asterisk after their name in the phone book saying they don't mind getting phone pitches.

Of course, Ohio Bell and fund-raisers and mass marketers don't like this idea. It will raise the price of doing business. "If you get one of these calls, just hang up," they reason.

That rationale evades the issue: Why should citizens like Durback be bothered in the first place? They shouldn't.

September 12, 1983

The Halle's murder

Yesterday, Mrs. Walter Halle came downtown to visit the store that once was the pendant in the glittering Halle's chain.

"I am so mad, I am just so mad," she said about the closing of the 90-year-old department store company that her family built into a Cleveland tradition.

"You know, I am going to get one of those plaques," the widow of Halle Brothers former chairman went on. "I am going to get one if I have to come down at midnight and take it off the wall."

The plaques, dozens of them, have been hanging for decades on the walls of Halle stores. The handsome wood plaques bear a caption, "A Leaf from our Policy." The text underneath the caption reads in part:

This establishment puts no premium on clever tricks or cute business practice. Be open, frank, above all, honest. Decide the simple law of right or wrong — then you can't go wrong.

Many Halle's employees wish their last, brief owners, Associated Investors Corp., had followed that advice. Nine weeks ago, its chairman, Jerome Schottenstein, vowed to maintain the Halle's tradition. He bought newspaper ads that said: "We believe, as much as you, in what Halle's has always been. We assure you that Halle's will remain a viable, quality name."

The stated plan was to close a couple of suburban stores, upgrade the merchandise, and rent out unneeded space in the downtown store. Two days ago, he announced the closing.

"I am disappointed in the way in which Halle's new owners lied to their customers and to the community," May Company President H. Gene Nau said yesterday. "I think they tried to save the Christmas season and then they pulled the plug."

This scathing criticism is not what you would expect from the head of a department store that is bound to pick up much of Halle's $70 million in annual sales.

Scarcely two hours before she heard the bad news, Halle's fashion director, Dixie Lee Davis, was in New York City, talking to a large clothing manufacturer about being bought out by Schottenstein's Associated Investors, which owns the Value City chain.

"It's the best thing," Davis told the manufacturer. "They will invest money in us and turn the merchandise around."

Then she and two other Halle's buyers heard the bad news.

"We went to a coffee shop on Seventh Avenue and just stared at each other," she said yesterday. "It seemed so unreal." Davis, a smartly dressed woman in her forties, lit a cigarette and surveyed the mess that was her office. "I'm packing up," she said sadly. "It will be thirty years in June.

"I was raised at Halle's. I was working here before I finished high school. I knew S. H. Halle, Walter Halle. Halle's was never just a store or just a job. It was family. . . .

"They didn't give us a chance," Davis said of the store's last owners. "They really don't know us. The time has been too short. . . . We were told, 'Don't go looking for jobs.' We all had such hope, and we believed them. We were so taken in."

Until the last decade, Halle's was Cleveland's finest department store, catering to the carriage trade with quality goods at higher prices. An old ad put it well: "Quiet good taste, whispers Halle's."

For three generations, Halle's set and maintained a caring and congenial atmosphere. Company loyalty was strong; its Twenty-Five Year Club had 873 members, a remarkable testament to its treatment of employees. Former employees might move on to better retailing jobs in Cleveland or New York or Chicago. Davis said they'd often visit and remark: "We don't have the same feeling where we work now. We miss that special relationship."

"I just cannot believe there won't be a Halle's," said Davis as she reached for a Kleenex on her desk to wipe away tears. "We worked on the bridal fair over the weekend. Everyone was so up and happy. In forty-eight hours, it's all changed."

Last week, she and many longtime employees went to the funeral of Chisholm Halle, the son of Walter and the grandson of Samuel H., Halle's co-founder.

"We said this would be the end of an era," Davis said. "We didn't know that next week it would be a complete end."

January 28, 1982

Unhappy money

At first, I was jealous when I heard that David DeVault, a 27-year-old bachelor from Chardon, had won the $7.8 million Ohio Lotto jackpot.

I had finally begun buying Ohio Lotto tickets, rationalizing that the gambling money went to taxes that helped educate school kids.

(Really, I had been seduced by greed and sloth. Hey, nobody's perfect.)

Anyway, I was jealous, until I talked yesterday to Helen Burnheimer, twenty-five, who grew up in North Royalton.

Helen won $1 million last year in the U-Haul Million Dollar Sweepstakes. She was getting welfare and living in Alliance, Ohio, at the time. She was separated from her husband and struggling to feed her two young girls.

One day last year, she got evicted. She rented a U-Haul trailer to move her raggedy belongings, unaware of the million-dollar giveaway.

A month or so later, Helen arrived at her apartment and spied a yellow notice taped to the door. Great, she thought, the electricity is being shut off.

It was a telegram from U-Haul. It said she had won a million bucks. Helen jumped up and down, screamed, laughed, cried, and called her friends and family.

U-Haul is paying her $50,000 a year for twenty years. When the check came, she went to an Alliance car dealer who sold her a new Corvette. Helen drove the lemon yellow sports car right out of the showroom.

Life is going to be great, she thought.

"For the first month," she said yesterday, "I was so depressed."

No wonder. Her estranged husband, who she said had abandoned her, showed up and said he was calling off their divorce.

Her friends treated her differently. Some demanded loans or outright gifts. Others thought she was getting too high class and snobby.

"All I have left are two real friends," Helen said. "[The others] were asking for money. They felt I owed it to them. That loss of friendship hurt me."

Salesmen besieged her apartment. Men wanted to marry her. One girlfriend asked her to be the godmother of her child. "In the next breath, she said I could buy her a brass crib," Helen recalled. "I would have bought her a crib if she needed one."

A so-called friend of Helen's fiancé asked him for money to fix a car. Her fiancé said no, and besides, the first check hadn't arrived.

The next day, the brother of the so-called friend beat up Helen's fiancé. "I got punched, too, trying to stop it," Helen said. "The police got involved. It was really ugly."

Someone vandalized her Corvette. People sent her threatening letters. She got an unlisted phone and moved. So people in the small town harassed her fiancé's mother, tying lawn chairs to her doors and breaking windows.

Helen said they were forced to move. They settled in North Royalton earlier this year. But her estranged husband and his family hounded her there.

Finally, Helen and her kids and boyfriend moved to a southern state, where they live in a $117,000 home.

"It's brought a lot of problems," she said about the million-dollar jackpot. "It's brought a lot of good, too. I've done stuff for the kids. They're kinda spoiled now. And I got out of debt, which had bothered me."

For David DeVault, the new millionaire from Chardon, Helen has some advice.

"Know who your friends are," she said. "Of course, you think you do. I hope, with him being young, he'll have a good head. I wish him the best of luck. I hope it works out.

"It's sad sometimes. It is. Money doesn't make you happy. There's a lot of snobby people. If you don't have money, so what? Sometimes I do wish I didn't win it. I get depressed and wish I was still poor.

"I guess I'm better off now, though," said Helen, who'd like to move back here someday. "I've got a secure future."

So for all you Ohio Lotto losers, buck up. Winning a fortune isn't all it's cracked up to be.

In fact, I urge you, for your mental and physical health, to refrain from buying Lotto tickets. It isn't worth losing your friends and being forced to move out of town.

If you see a guy buying a Lotto ticket who resembles the little mugshot with this column, don't jump to conclusions. Hey, a lot of people look alike.

December 22, 1983

6
WORDSMITHS

Changing fortunes

The time is the late 1960s and the place is Garry Trudeau's comic strip.

Three Yale football players, in quest of female companionship, are traveling by car to a college mixer.

Two are sitting in the front seat. One says to other: "Hey, we're three famous football players. Think anybody will recognize us?"

"No," says one. He turns and addresses the third guy, who sits in the back seat.

"Hey, B.D., what do you think?"

The reader sees quarterback B.D. for the first time. He's wearing dress clothes and his football helmet.

"Oh, I don't know about that," B.D. says.

Brian Dowling, the Cleveland football hero on whom Trudeau based the *Doonesbury* character B.D., said yesterday he never wore a football helmet to a mixer. Unlike B.D., Dowling said he's not a bighead. Nor did he grouse about campus wimps, peace demonstrators or longhairs.

"B.D. didn't have much political identification when we were in school," said Dowling, thirty-five, who graduated from Yale in 1969. "Trudeau developed him as a stereotypical football-player, rightwing hawk type. It didn't parallel my life at all."

Like Trudeau's characterizations of a lame-brained Ronald Reagan, the B.D. character may not be flattering to Dowling, who quarterbacked St. Ignatius High School and Yale University to championships.

But Dowling really doesn't mind. He's like most of *Doonesbury*'s 65 million readers. He's going to miss Trudeau's comic strip. Trudeau is taking a 20-month vacation and his parting *Doonesbury* was published yesterday.

"I enjoy it," Dowling said. "He [Trudeau] is very clever, and he's been very successful with it. I've never been offended by any of them. I've been able to laugh at myself.

"One of the messages he's trying to bring across is no matter what your position is in life, you can't take yourself too seriously."

Dowling certainly was taken seriously in Cleveland. He electrified audiences as no high school athlete has since. In 1964, playing before 41,183 at the Stadium, St. Ignatius' Dowling ran for one and passed for four touchdowns, demolishing Benedictine High School 48-6 and clinching a city championship.

As football captain at Yale, calling his own plays from the huddle, he and backfield teammate Calvin Hill led the Bulldogs to two consecutive Ivy League championships. The reserved, conservative kid from the Midwest became a big man on campus.

"I got a lot of publicity," Dowling said mildly.

He met Trudeau in person on campus only once. Trudeau's comic strip — called *Bull Tales* when it appeared in the *Yale Daily News* — was an instant smash.

"Interest almost became addictive," Dowling recalled. "He began satirizing a lot of publicity I was getting."

As fast as Trudeau's star shot up, Dowling's fizzled out.

By 1977, Trudeau was a media superstar. Some of his cartoon strips were judged by a few lily-livered newspaper editors to be too controversial for print. Readers by the thousands complained of the censorship.

Then Trudeau married a fellow media superstar, NBC *Today Show* host Jane Pauley, and he settled into a life-style almost as secretive as that of the great writer J.D. Salinger.

In contrast, when Dowling popped up as B.D. in a 1977 comic strip, Trudeau portrayed him sitting on the bench of the Washington Redskins with running back Calvin Hill. Which is what Dowling and Hill were doing in real life.

At the time, Dowling had played for a string of pro teams. He always seemed to end up playing behind high-priced quarterbacks. Coaches didn't like his wobbly passes, although when he did get a chance to play, Dowling had an uncanny knack for putting points on the scoreboard.

Dowling made it back out on the football field this season — as color commentator at five college games for CBS sports. He lives with his wife in Marblehead, Massachusetts, looking after a real estate investment or two and working on a cable television venture.

Two months ago, during the football strike, Dowling clipped out a *Doonesbury* cartoon starring B.D. and mailed it to Trudeau, who lives in Manhattan.

The former big man on campus politely asked the once-obscure cartoonist if he could spare the original.

"He sent me the original of the strip," Dowling said happily. "He inscribed it. It was very nice."

January 3, 1983

Street intellectual

". . . Inside of a Barricade were several thousands of Men, Women and Children. They were moving restlessly among the trampled weeds, which were clotted with Watermelon Rinds, Chicken Bones, Straw and torn Paper Bags." — George Ade, *Fables in American Slang,* 1899.

Harvey Pekar, the street-corner intellectual of Coventry Road, was on his way to the Coventry Street Fair yesterday. He wore second-hand slacks and a tattered tank-style undershirt.

"I feel like a prophet without honor in my own town," Harvey said. "My new book jus' came out. Number 7. I think it's my best yet."

Harvey's books, *American Splendor* Nos. 1-7, are collections of his real-life experiences shaped into vignettes and illustrated in a comic book format.

His stories, everyday incidents of working people, are often depressing on the surface, but ironical and humorous underneath. Harvey's writing is influenced by George Ade, the turn-of-the-century humorist, newspaper columnist and realist writer.

Harvey's work has been the toast of New York writers and critics and a movie producer or two. But in Cleveland, Harvey is known mostly as the guy in the undershirt who hangs out on Coventry and listens to the old-timers at Irv's Delicatessen tell stories about their lives.

He may be a prophet without honor, a serious writer without acclaim, but he is used to silence by now.

"I don't expect nuthin' out of this town," Harvey said yesterday. "I'm not bitter about it."

Thus they wove and interwove in the Smoky Oven. The Whim-
per or the faltering wail, of children, the quavering sighs of over-
laced Women, and the long drawn profanity of Men — these were
what (he) heard as he looked upon the Suffering Throng.

Harvey, forty-two, walked to the street fair with Sue Cavey,
twenty-nine, a former circus cook and now an art student. She
had illustrated a few stories in *American Splendor* No. 7.

The Coventry Street Fair was swelling by the minute with aging
hippies in cutoffs and baggy sun dresses, senior citizens in cheap
sunglasses, high school kids in preppie attire, and homeowners
pushing strollers and middle age.

The Mr. Stress Blues Band began wailing in the parking lot behind the Coventry Beverage Store. Nearby, trim young women in
bright tights and leotards were bopping out a Jazzercise demon-
stration.

The wind whipped the crowd with the pungent smoke from the
fires of the street vendors who sold barbecued ribs, shish kebab
and hamburgers.

Harvey walked into Coventry Books, the bookstore. He checked
with owner Ellie Strong. He wanted cash for the one hundred copies of *American Splendor* No. 7 the store had agreed to take.

"They're selling, but not as well as I expected," she said.

"I didn't expect anything," Harvey replied.

She handed him $80. "I'll give you the $20 tomorrow," she said.

Harvey used seventy-five cents of his $80 to buy some falafel,
deep-fried balls of dough and peas, a Middle East specialty, from
a street vendor.

Harvey works as a clerk at a hospital. He is a Jack Benny
cheapskate except when it comes to jazz records and *American
Splendor.* Each issue costs him about $7,000. He writes the words
and pays free-lance artists to draw the illustrations.

He loses money. But it doesn't seem to bother him anymore.
"As long as I get recognition from the people who know what I'm
doing — that's what matters," he said. "The thing does not have
commercial appeal. I got three bites from movie producers. But
they all fell through."

"Is this a new wrinkle on Dante's Inferno?" he asked the Man
on the Gate, who wore a green Badge marked "Marshall," and was
taking tickets.

"No, sir; this is a County Fair," was the reply.

"Why do the People congregate in the Weeds and allow the sun to warp them?"

"Because everybody does it."

. . . Moral: People who expect to be Luny will find it safer to travel in a Bunch.

July 12, 1982

A dandy writer

Hurtling north on I-71 yesterday, Tom Wolfe peered out a limousine window and commented on the graceful, arching street lamps.

"You see those lights?" he asked. "They're all over. They link America. I wonder who's the architect." Pause. "There must be a big switch where they turn them on."

Uh, how's that, Tom? Here's one of America's finest reporters, the flashy writer who knocked 1960s magazine writing on its stodgy behind, the scourge of intellectuals, a guy who just cashed in on $1.1 million for paperback and movie rights to his current bestseller, *The Right Stuff,* and he's talking about a bunch of . . . street lights?

Yes, indeed. If it's not street lights, then it might be the Appalachian drawl of test pilot Chuck Yeager or the appetizers at Leonard Bernstein's high-society fundraiser for the Black Panthers or the silicone-inflated breasts of topless dancer Carol Doda.

Tom Wolfe writes abundantly about this arcane stuff, the minute details that make up our popular culture. And in doing so, as *Newsweek* once put it, Wolfe "captures the seeping miasma of madness that is drifting over the modern world. . . . Wolfe is in the style of the great American Fictionalists from Stephen Crane to Ring Lardner to Hemingway to John O'Hara to Mailer."

Wolfe does not write about "Big Issues" — the state of the nation, the quest for oil, the nuclear power controversy. Instead he writes of the Third Great Awakening, his term for the proliferation of religious groups in the 1970s, a phenomenon he predicts will carry over into the '80s.

"It's just beginning," he said. "There are forty gods out there prancing around. There's a religious upsurge. There's searching.

Running is a religion now. Weightlifters, they talk about 'the white moment' . . . ."

Wolfe is a dandy whose flashy suits are ideal self-promotion. Yesterday, he wore light gray doeskin gloves, a white serge suit with blue-and-black pinstripes, a vest with a collar, a blue shirt, a skinny white tie with black polka dots, and white doeskin wing tips. And on his head: a powder-blue, custom-made streamlined fedora.

What else can this reporter-forecaster tell us on the eve of the 1980s?

The next decade, Wolfe believes, will continue to see married couples placing less importance on having offspring. He calls it "the breakdown in the belief of serial immortality."

"You have married couples talking coldly about the cost of having children. The birthrate now, I believe, is below the replacement level. In Europe, they worry about this."

But the '80s will also see a rise in "the belief in blood," the nobility of one's ethnic group, says Wolfe. Since people aren't embracing organized religion as tightly, they are replacing it with belief in blood.

But Wolfe does not think times will be bleak.

"We've had a 40-year boom," Wolfe pointed out. "Western Europe has had prosperity beyond what was dreamed of a century ago. Wealth has filtered down to the working class at all levels.

"And socialism is finished, absolutely finished, because of the discovery of concentration camps. You can't find a detour around the concentration camps. Everytime a regime begins, they say 'Where are the concentration camps?' And they're always there. Which is all very good for the West. It will be a great period to write about."

Wolfe started writing after earning a Ph.D. in American Studies at Yale University. He was hired as a copy boy at *The New York Daily News* because an editor wanted a doctor to hustle his cokes. As a cub reporter in Springfield, Massachusetts, he chased fires, working nights and right up to deadline, infatuated with the newspaper game, as it used to be called before journalism schools came along and made things serious.

Later, he was Latin American correspondent for *The Washington Post,* and finally feature writer at *The New York Herald Tribune.* Here he achieved his stylistic breakthrough with point-of-view and wild punctuation, calling it New Journalism.

Wolfe is widely imitated today, in many cases very well, by

writers at *The Village Voice* and *Rolling Stone.*

Other progenitors of New Journalism include Norman Mailer with *Armies of the Night* and Truman Capote with *In Cold Blood.*

Wolfe was somewhat surprised that reviewers felt his portrait of John Glenn in *The Right Stuff* was an unsympathetic one. "I guess I feel a kinship with Glenn although we're very very different," he said. Wolfe added that he admired Glenn's combination of piety and aggressiveness, an ideal of his Presbyterianism, that makes him a sort of "secular saint."

"I may be going out on a limb, but this was the strength of the Midwest," Wolfe said. "A man like Glenn is a rarity, a genuinely straight arrow."

Someday, Wolfe may write another book about astronauts and moon walks. He had planned to include all this in *The Right Stuff,* but narrowed his topic.

First, he'd like to write a novel, about the manners and morals of New York City, kind of like Thackeray's *Vanity Fair.* Or maybe a book about high school students. "I haven't seen much written from the student's side. I bet Cleveland would be good for that."

But first, Wolfe must polish off a commitment to *Harpers* to write a sequel to his controversial piece on pop art called "The Painted Word." The sequel will focus on architecture, and maybe even have a few pages about highway lamp poles.

October 30, 1979

Heller strikes gold

You," Joseph Heller's mother would tell him, "have a twisted brain."

"I think I do," Heller admitted yesterday. "But her own brain was twisted, too. We had a cousin, a gross looking girl. My mother would say, 'She's so homely, there's better looking at the Barnum and Bailey.' "

This kind of perverse, bleak humor streaks through the novels of Joseph Heller, arguably America's best-selling "serious" novelist.

His *Catch-22* satirized war and 1950s American society; it sold eight million copies and its title has become part of our language.

Something Happened, declared by critics as a literary *tour de force,* took Heller thirteen years to write and dismissed jealous barbs that he was a one-novel phenomenon.

Now, behold *Good as Gold,* Heller's third novel, which this week is No. 1 on the best-sellers list. Simon & Schuster paid him more than $1 million in advance royalties before he put pen to paper.

The novel, a critical as well as a financial success, has done to Washington bureaucracy what *Catch-22* did to the military.

Heller, with a full halo of gray curls, looked fit given his 56-years and his notorious weakness for food, be it Chinese or Jewish. He was in town as part of his eleven-city book-promotion tour.

Authors as rich and talented as Heller don't have to suffer promotion tours like some washed up country star making a string of one-night stands in backwoods honky tonks.

Heller would rather be with Shirley, his wife of thirty-three years, or having dinner with the Gang of Four, a group of friends that sometimes includes pal Mel Brooks, maker of funny movies.

Cleveland is an important book market, Heller acknowledged as he walked to a waiting limousine. Simon & Schuster's biggest seller since Woodward and Bernstein, Heller was given star treatment.

"I don't mind them [book tours]," Heller said, a remark blasphemous to some "serious" writers who feel plugging their own books is unbecoming to the art.

"I actually work harder once I've written the book," the author remarked. "Then I can edit it for eight hours a day and read the galleys for twelve hours a day."

Simply put, Heller is a perfectionist. So much so that the thirteen years it took him to follow up *Catch-22* (1961) with *Something Happened* could have stretched into decades. He would rewrite a chapter, then two weeks later throw that out and start over, rewriting, rewriting, never letting go . . . until his editor stepped in and put an end to the dilly-dallying.

Good as Gold tells of a New York professor, Bruce Gold, who hates his Jewish family and wants to find fame, fortune and beautiful lovers in Washington where an old college chum is a presidential aide.

Gold is offered the job of "unnamed spokesman" with no salary but $1,000 a day in expenses. Gold is also writing a book about being Jewish in America and despises Henry Kissinger as the archetypal *schmuck*.

"I don't think about Kissinger at all," Heller said yesterday. "I haven't seen his name in the papers. Either he's writing a book or he's got cancer."

Many people find *Good as Gold* deeply disturbing. The book portrays a society that is going crazy. Everybody learns to accept disorder as order.

This response pleased Heller.

"When I wrote *Catch-22* I didn't know I had the ability to be funny," he said. "With *Good as Gold* I didn't know I had the power to be so touching."

Heller likens the mechanics of his writing to memorizing. He will hear a funny line or sentence and work from there. He says he cannot sit down and write a one-liner.

For example, Heller and one of his Gang of Four buddies were walking in New York City and spied a shop selling artifical limbs.

"My friend has a grisly sense of humor," Heller recounted. "He was babbling on" — Heller goes into a salesman-like spiel — " 'Have I got an arm for you! Hey, where did you get that eye?' "

Heller included this in his novel. His mother's remark about the homely cousin also found its way into Heller's work.

Heller's work is noted for its lack of plot and by lots of eccentric characters. His novels nearly defy translation into movies.

"I think there's a movie in here," Heller said, holding a copy of his new novel. "Mike Nichols [he did *The Graduate*] and I have had many discussions about this book. He saw large parts of it before it was finished. But he's so busy with so many other things."

As for his next book, Heller said he has no idea, not an inkling, about what it will concern. "I usually have no idea for five to eight months after a book is published. So I'm not worried." An unspoken "yet" seemed to linger in the air.

Heller is a worrier. Remarked his close friend Mario Puzo (bestselling author of *The Godfather* and *Fools Die*): "I never knew somebody so determined to be unhappy. If he's happy, he gets unhappy."

Heller has been described as a hidden man who masks his feelings with mockery and anger, whose true feelings are known to only a handful of intimate friends. He is also a compulsive dieter and jogger and fears the loss of his talents.

Death and growing old worry him, too. Death is a theme in all his novels. And *Good as Gold* tells of the plight of Bruce Gold's 83-year-old father, a crotchety, evil man who bullies his middle-aged children. Yet at the end of the book, the reader feels a bit of remorse for the man whose children can't do anything with him so try to get him to move to a condominium in Florida, banished to loneliness.

"I hate being alone," Heller said. "Last night in Detroit had to be one of the loneliest nights in my life. I didn't know anybody. I had a big dinner and drank too much."

"Tonight I'm going to a dinner party a bookstore is having for me. I'll have a couple of scotches. It will be OK unless they want to talk about serious literary things. I don't know anything about that."

April 17, 1979

Johnny Deadline

Terrorists murder Marines in Beirut. The United States invades a banana republic. Headlines trumpet death, destruction, dissent. The world's in a tangle, and roving reporter Bob Greene . . . well, he checks into the Holiday Inn Rockside.

Greene was visiting Cleveland to promote *American Beat,* a collection of his columns for *Esquire* and *The Chicago Tribune.*

How do you feel being stuck on a book tour when big news is breaking elswhere? he was asked.

"How can you write anything about that unless you're down there?" he replied. "Ninety per cent of the columns this week will be about the same thing: Grenada or Beirut. Most newspaper columnists read the front page of *The New York Times* and pontificate about that."

Greene does not digest *The New York Times,* suck on his thumb while pondering the troubled cosmos, then regurgitate a cud of words *à la* Joseph Kraft and his brethren.

Rather, Greene is a storyteller in the Ben Hecht mold, a spinner of small human dramas that, when they're good (which is often), reveal a larger truth. In *American Beat,* his seventh book, Greene tells of a career woman jilted at the altar; a millworker fighting in the Tough Man contest; a renegade actor trying out for a part; paying a visit to a high school sweetheart nearly twenty years later; watching a young woman have an abortion.

When Greene latches onto the Big Story of the Day, which he does infrequently, he invariably comes away with an angle that leaves other reporters asking, "Why didn't I think of that?"

Greene, nicknamed "Johnny Deadline," was a boy wonder. He started writing his column for *The Chicago Sun-Times* at twenty-three. In 1980, after winning nearly every reporting award in

Chicago, he moved to *The Tribune*. He is syndicated in 120 newspapers and writes a monthly column for *Esquire* called "American Beat." He is a correspondent for ABC's "Nightline," and reaches millions of viewers.

As journalist Tom Wolfe put it, "Bob Greene is a virtuoso of things that bring journalism alive."

Greene, thirty-six, walked into the Holiday Inn lobby one recent night. He was tired. No wonder. Four columns a week, a monthly *Esquire* piece and two or more reports for "Nightline" keep him going up to eighty hours a week.

He is not your TV pretty boy. His speech is steeped in the Buckeye twang of Columbus, where he was reared. He is average in height, weight and looks. He is lousy at small talk. You get the idea he's rather shy.

So this is the tiger who got convicted mass murderer Richard Speck's first public admission of guilt; the reporter who scored exclusives with Patty Hearst and Richard Nixon when both were dodging the press?

Yes, and there's a reason. Greene is fiercely ambitious. He possesses a more than healthy-sized ego.

Greene told a story. He was twenty-five. He wanted to cover the 1972 presidential campaign for *The Chicago Sun-Times*. His editors said no. Too expensive.

So go-getter Greene lined up a book contract and hit the trail, paying his expenses with $10,000 of his savings. *The Sun-Times* gladly printed the columns he turned out. Then he shaped them into a book, *Running: A Nixon-McGovern Campaign Journal*.

"My ambition was so great, I was willing to do that," he said.

What makes Johnny Deadline run?

"It's a combination of pathological curiosity and intense fear of being wrong," Greene said. "Not only will I make that extra call, I'll make an extra twelve calls."

Chicago has been the main bullring for columnists: Greene, Mike Royko, Roger Simon, Ann Landers, Irv Kupcinet, John Schulian; the list goes on. What makes Chicago such a breeding ground?

"What would draw a potentially terrific columnist to *The New York Times* or *The Washington Post*?" Greene asked. "They wouldn't let him have his leash. In Chicago, they let a columnist be a columnist. They don't want editorial columnists. He doesn't have to look over his shoulder to please management."

Greene went to dinner. He had two vodka gimlets, fried perch and french fries. Then he went to bed early on the night of two of the biggest breaking news stories of the year.

That's Bob Greene.

"I am neither pundit nor philosopher," he explained in *American Beat*. "I try to be a storyteller; I try to go out and explore something that interests me, and then — after hanging around and watching and listening and asking questions — I try to give the reader some sense of what it was like to be there. . . .

"Those are the kinds of things that 'don't really qualify as 'news,' but that seem to me to have as much to do with the way we live as most of the events that warrant bold banner headlines."

October 29, 1983

A fourth generation Clevelander and graduate of St. Ignatius High School, James Neff has worked at *The Plain Dealer* for the past six years. He attended the University of Notre Dame and holds a masters degree in American Civilization from the University of Texas at Austin. His first newspaper job was at *The Austin American-Statesman*. Neff lives in Lakewood with his wife, Maureen Murphy, a lawyer.